A sure sign of the apocalypse . . .

The dead man stood with his head tilted to the side at such a sharp angle that it nearly rested on his right shoulder. His mouth hung open, and the tip of his swollen, pale tongue jutted between his teeth. Grains of sand from Harley and Kenyon's attempt at burial still clung to the skin of the man's face. His eyes were a milky blue—as cold and empty as a mackerel under plastic wrap at the grocery store.

Harley's legs seemed to turn to liquid. She stumbled back, keeping the beam of her flashlight fixed on the dead man's face. She tried to call for Kenyon, but all that came out of her mouth was a low, dry sob.

Something shifted below the skin of the dead man's face. One of the lifeless eyes bulged from its socket. A silver snake slipped out of the gap in the corner of the eye. The snake was no bigger around than a strand of spaghetti, with two pinpoint black eyes at one end. Its head pulled out a few inches, swung back and forth through the air for a moment, then snapped back like a rubber band.

"What . . . ," breathed Harley. "What are you?"

Don't miss any books in this thrilling series:

EXTREME ZONE™

Available from ARCHWAY Paperbacks

EXTREME ZONE™

DEAD
END

M.C. SUMNER

AN ARCHWAY PAPERBACK
Published by POCKET BOOKS

New York   London   Toronto   Sydney   Tokyo   Singapore

AN ARCHWAY PAPERBACK *Original*

 An Archway Paperback published by
POCKET BOOKS, a division of Simon & Schuster Inc.
1230 Avenue of the Americas, New York, NY 10020

Produced by Daniel Weiss Associates, Inc., New York

Copyright © 1998 by Daniel Weiss Associates, Inc., and
Mark C. Sumner
Cover art copyright © 1998 by Daniel Weiss Associates, Inc.

ISBN: 0-671-01414-5

First Archway Paperback printing February 1998

10 9 8 7 6 5 4 3 2 1

AN ARCHWAY PAPERBACK and colophon are
registered trademarks of Simon & Schuster Inc.

EXTREME ZONE and the EXTREME ZONE logo are
trademarks of Daniel Weiss Associates, Inc.

Printed in the U.S.A.

IL 7+

PROLOGUE

The ax blade bit hard into the chunk of hickory. Slivers of pale wood arced into the air and tumbled like glitter. There was a satisfying crack, and the length of wood split cleanly up the middle to fall into two wedge-shaped pieces.

Noah Templer lowered the ax to the ground and paused to wipe the sweat from his brow. He pushed a stray lock of hair back under the brim of his floppy wool hat. Noah's hair had gotten increasingly shaggy over the last months. He had done his best to chop it himself, but the results were not exactly stylish. After years of wearing his hair short for basketball and track, the increasing length felt strange. He looked down at his rough-hewn leather trousers and homemade vest that left the center of his chest bare. Weeks in the sun had darkened his skin, and hard work had built muscle on his slender frame. Noah flexed a callused hand and wondered how many of his teammates back in Stone Harbor would recognize him now.

The sun was almost directly overhead and the temperature was warm, but Noah wasn't fooled. It might be still fall, but every now and then Noah caught a taste of winter in the air. He suspected it was going to be a hard, cold season. There was more than a cord of wood stacked against the rear wall of the cabin Noah called home, but he was pretty sure all that wood and

1

more would be needed for him to stay warm against the coming snows.

A small chevron of geese appeared from the north, skimming over the treetops, and flew honking across the valley where Noah was working. He tipped back the brim of his hat and stared up to watch them pass. Noah frowned. Something was wrong with the geese. They *looked* all right, with their long white necks and dangling feet, but they didn't *move* well. Their flight was fluttering and frantic—more like bats than geese.

"Hold up!" he shouted to the birds.

The geese froze in the air. They hung in the sky as though suspended from invisible wires or imbedded in a huge block of crystal.

Noah rose up to meet them, floating through the sunlit air as if his body were filled with helium. When he got close to the frozen flock, he saw the problem at once. The wings were bending too far. He was almost certain that real geese held their wings stiffer.

Holding out one finger toward the geese, Noah tried to imagine how the internal structure of the wing should look. For the hundredth time that week he wished he had paid more attention in science class— animals were *complex*. Finally, when the changes to the geese seemed as successful as he could manage, Noah lowered himself back to the ground.

"All right," he said. "Go ahead."

The geese began to fly again. This time their movement was smoother and their flapping seemed less frenzied.

Noah was pleased. The motion of the geese was still not quite perfect, but it was much better. He would work on them again later—after his chores were done.

He raised his heavy ax and began to split another section from the hickory tree. Of course, Noah didn't really *need* to chop the wood. He could have warmed up the nights or even reversed the seasons with little more effort than it had taken to fix the wobbly flight of the geese. But he hated to interfere unless something was actually broken.

Creating this world had taken a tremendous effort, and keeping it running smoothly required a considerable amount of thought. Noah knew from experience that changing anything around him could cause a whole series of problems. It was like pulling one string in a complex tapestry—you never knew what other threads might unravel. Noah could put everything back in order, but it took time and effort. If he tried to change anything as complicated as the seasons, he might soon find that chopping wood was a whole lot easier than fixing the damage his meddling caused.

Something shifted at the corner of Noah's eye.

Noah raised his head and looked across the valley. The movement had surprised him, but he wasn't really alarmed. In addition to the birds there was quite a collection of animals around the valley: foxes, raccoons, deer, even a small black bear. None of them was particularly dangerous, so he had no reason to be afraid. Noah was more interested in seeing what the creature was and if it was working well in this tiny, artificial world.

On the surface the valley looked the same as it had for months. A cluster of wooden cabins centered around a stone-lined well. Farther back was a small blacksmith's shop, a large barn, and a couple of incomplete fences. Cedar shingles had rained down the side of the barn and lay in gray drifts against the sides. The fences were already going to ruin. When winter came, Noah expected at least half the buildings would fall.

Not too long ago every cabin had been full, and there had been plans to build more. But one by one the other residents of the little community had slipped away, leaving Noah alone to tend the miniature world.

Whatever had moved, it wasn't moving now. Noah decided that he must have seen a falling leaf or a piece of the crumbling buildings on its way to the ground. He was about to go back to his rail splitting when once again he spotted something sliding along at the very limits of his vision. Noah spun around rapidly, and this time he managed to glimpse a small, brown thing dart behind one of the cabins.

Noah frowned. The creature might have been one of the raccoons, but it hadn't looked right. It wasn't just broken like the geese—this thing hadn't looked familiar at all. Still holding the ax, he walked toward the place where he had seen the brown form disappear. He was halfway there when the brown thing went skittering across the gap between two buildings like a mad cartoon rabbit. As it zipped into the woods it actually seemed to *blur*.

I'm going nuts, Noah thought. That's what happens to people who stay alone for too long—especially people who are already living in a world that only exists inside their own head. He smiled to himself. I don't have to go nuts. I already am nuts.

He dropped the ax onto the mossy ground and walked casually toward the patch of trees where he had last seen the creature. He had no reason to be afraid. After all, it was his world.

At first Noah saw nothing unusual in the forest. There were only the rough, lichen-stained trunks and a fringe of high grass. The brown thing had vanished. Noah shook his head and turned back toward the cabins.

And then at the very edge of his vision he saw it. This time it didn't move. It was no bigger than a five-year-old child and thin as starvation. Its skin was a dry, grocery-bag brown that blended well with the fallen leaves. It had a rough texture like sandpaper and knobby bumps of what might have been matted hair clumped along the slope of its shoulders.

Slowly Noah turned to face the thing. He half expected it to disappear—to turn back into a clump of shrubs transformed by a trick of the light and a touch of fear—but the thing remained stubbornly real. It had no face. There was a head, but it was only a misshapen lump of brown skin without a trace of mouth, nose, ears, or eyes.

"What are you?" Noah whispered.

The brown thing raised its arms. Its fingers were terribly long and knotted with far more joints than any human digit. It pointed the skeletal fingers at Noah and rustled them like dry twigs in a breeze.

Noah stepped back. There had been visitors to his private world, but none like this. He wondered if the thing might be the product of one of his own nightmares. Maybe in his growing madness he had started to carve a race of terrible children. He wished that he still had the ax.

"What are you?" he asked again. "Who made you?"

The brown thing let out a hiss like a basket full of vipers.

Noah stumbled over his own feet and fell backward. He climbed up onto his hands and knees. The brown thing had run over to Noah and now peered down at him, its terrible fingers twisting in the air inches from Noah's face.

The thing was small, but that didn't stop Noah from being horrified. The creature's movements were lightning fast, and it was utterly alien.

Noah pushed his heels against the ground and scooted backward over the dead grass. The creature stayed put, wiggling its hands and tilting its featureless face from side to side.

"What do you want?" Noah asked in a shaky voice. "Why are you here?"

The creature raised its twig fingers above its head, then brought them down in a slash. As the long hands cut through the space in front of it there was a sound like cloth being ripped. Its fingers left a trail of flat featureless gray trimmed with sparkling static in their wake. With a second swipe of its hands it tore the patch of gray wider. Then, with a final sharp hiss, the thing stepped into the rip in the air and vanished.

Noah struggled to his feet and stepped carefully toward the splotch of gray that remained hanging a few feet off the ground. While the static around the edges still held color and motion, the area in the center of the tear was utterly dead. Noah had seen this washed-out, empty color before—it was the stuff of the sphere. Before he had summoned this make-believe world from his own memories, he had floated for countless hours in that endless wash of gray.

Slowly the wound in the air began to heal itself.

The sparkling static spilled into the gray, and the colors of the ground and forest filled in around the edge. In a few seconds the wound had closed up entirely.

It took a lot longer than a few seconds for Noah's heart and breathing to return to normal. In all the time he had been in the sphere, he had never seen anything like the brown creature.

Things are changing, he thought. It was definitely a change for the worse.

After a few minutes he went back to his ax and returned to chopping wood. But he had only been working for a little while before he noticed more movement in the silent village.

This time he didn't have to look hard—the whole village was moving. Grass and trees and cabins all swayed and bent and distorted as a wave passed across the world. Noah thought it was like watching a man walking behind a tapestry, rippling the design.

More like an elephant, he amended after a moment. Whatever was causing the world to stretch and waver, it was far larger than a man. The distortion passed over the village and through the forest and vanished over a line of distant hills. Then the hills themselves vanished, leaving behind a patch of gray that was slowly filled in by sky and earth.

Noah looked at the ax in his hand, then let it slip to the ground. There was no longer any point in chopping wood.

Things *were* changing. The little world had been his home for months, but he was quite sure it wasn't going to last much longer. Long before winter set in, either Noah would somehow escape the sphere or his world would be gone.

**ONE**

Kathleen "Harley" Davisidaro lifted her shovel and heaved another scoop of sand into the grave. The damp grains struck the green canvas tarpaulin that was wrapped around the dead body and slid down the stiff cloth with an odd, hollow hiss that raised the hairs on the back of Harley's neck. Grave digging was definitely not her favorite occupation. She pushed the blade of her shovel into the ground and leaned against the handle.

"Are you sure we're doing the right thing?" she asked.

On the other side of the grave Kenyon Moor worked his shovel with mechanical steadiness. He glanced at Harley. Sweat ran through his dark hair and trickled down his forehead. His handsome, even features appeared calm, but there seemed to be a shadow around Kenyon's dark gray eyes.

"No," he replied. "In fact, I'm sure it's *not* the right thing." The muscles of his shoulders and arms knotted under his black sweater as he lifted a fresh load of earth and threw it into the grave. "But right or wrong, it's just something we have to do."

Harley nodded grimly. She gripped her shovel and pressed it down into the soft ground. But before she could move another scoop of sand, an electric tingle crawled up her spine. The wooden handle slipped from her fingers.

"Someone's out there," she whispered.

Kenyon didn't pause in his shoveling. "What?"

Harley shivered and hugged her arms around herself. "Something's wrong," she said. "It's like . . . it's like . . ."

"Like what?" Kenyon asked between scoops.

"I don't know." Harley's erratic mental powers had never been particularly reliable. She definitely felt *something*. It was as if she could sense the weight of a hundred unseen eyes staring at her. Staring from the dunes. Staring from the empty house. Staring from the grave. There was absolutely no sign of anyone watching, but Harley couldn't shake the tight, itching sensation between her shoulder blades.

Kenyon paused for a moment. "You okay?"

Harley nodded quickly. "Yeah," she said. "I'll be fine."

Without another word Kenyon returned to his work.

Harley craned her neck and looked around. She wasn't ready to confess her fear to Kenyon, but if she had learned anything over the last few months, it was not to ignore her instincts. She scanned her surroundings, looking for anything strange.

On her left, Kenyon's huge mansion loomed above a grove of wind-twisted cedars. A thick lawn spread like a carpet from the base of the old house. At one time the hedges that walled in the edges of the property had been neat and evenly clipped, but Kenyon hadn't been paying a lot of attention to keeping the place well-groomed.

Beyond the ragged shrubbery the lawn thinned quickly to sparse brown clumps of grass wedged in rolling gray sand dunes. The dunes crouched in rows down to the edge of the highway, then rose again on the other side of the road to reach the rocky Atlantic shore. The beach was deserted. The late afternoon sun cast a varnish of orange light over the whole scene. Chill, damp winds blew up the slope, and seagulls wheeled slowly against the darkening sky.

In between the house and the sea, the shallow grave sat like an open wound. The grass and low hummocks of sand would hide the grave from a few yards away, but from where Harley stood, it was all too exposed. Despite the nearness of Kenyon's expensive house, the makeshift burial ground seemed lonely and desolate.

Harley frowned. It was a gloomy, gray landscape, but if somebody was hiding out there, they were doing a very good job. Still, the feeling of being watched wouldn't go away. *You're just being paranoid*, she told herself. Less than forty-eight hours had passed since she had been kidnapped by the group called Unit 17. Kenyon, along with her best friend, Dee Janes, had helped free Harley from Unit 17, but she still felt more than a little uneasy. *Just because you're paranoid doesn't mean they're not out to get you*, she reminded herself.

Harley bent and picked up her shovel. "I just wish we didn't have to do this," she said.

Kenyon snorted. "What other choice is there?"

Harley shrugged and looked down at the half-buried body. She had never seen the man alive. According to the papers they had found near the body, the man had information about the secret organizations called Umbra and Unit 17. But which of the organizations—if either—the man belonged to was a mystery. They could only guess that he had come to

Kenyon's huge house to get information from the computer system inside and perhaps to kill Harley. Some of the papers that the man had been carrying concerned trading information on Harley. It wasn't clear how the dead man was involved in that deal, but Harley suspected he hadn't come to give her a bouquet of flowers.

Not that it mattered. Someone else had killed the unknown agent before he ever got a shot at her. When Kenyon had found the body lying on the soft lawn outside the house, the man had already been dead for hours.

Despite everything that had happened over the past weeks, Harley's first thought had been to call the police. Dee had talked her out of it. Dee's father was the local police chief. If the investigation of the body would go no further than Dee's father, everything probably would have been all right. But Dee had warned that unidentified dead bodies were just the kind of thing that would bring investigators from the state patrol—and maybe even the FBI.

That kind of attention was definitely something both Kenyon and Harley wanted to avoid. The paramilitary group known as Unit 17 had filled Harley's record with so many phony crimes, she was forced to go under a false name. If anyone checked too closely into her past, she would be spending a lot of time in a nice small cell. And Kenyon was wrapping up a legal battle with his brother over the multimillion-dollar estate of their parents. Explaining the presence of a dead man at the house was not likely to be very helpful in winning his case.

Harley swallowed hard. Kenyon's right, she thought. There's nothing else we can do. She raised the shovel and dropped a fresh load of sand onto the canvas over the man's face.

The body was almost covered and the grave nearly filled when Harley heard the crunch of tires rolling up the long gravel driveway toward the house. She raised her head and squinted against the afternoon sun. Through rows of tall shrubs she could see a blue-and-white police car slowly approaching up the sloping drive.

"Uh-oh," Harley warned. "Looks like we've got company." She dropped her shovel beside the grave and rubbed her hands against her jeans.

Kenyon glanced toward the car and scowled. "Stall them. I'll get this finished as fast as I can." He pushed his shovel into the ground and heaved more sand into the grave.

Harley's heart pounded as she hurried around the mansion to meet the car. Kenyon and the grave were just out of sight behind the building. If the police searched, they would spot the makeshift burial ground in a matter of seconds.

The police car cleared a small rise and rolled up to the house. Harley let out a sigh of relief as she saw that the vehicle was from the Stone Harbor Police Department. Chief Janes knew about the way the group Unit 17 had tried to make Harley look like a criminal, and he knew something about the strange things that had been going on. If there was one policeman in the world who wasn't after her, it was Chief Janes.

Even so, Harley didn't relax completely. As understanding as he was, she doubted that even Mr. Janes would like the idea of burying a dead body in the side yard.

Harley spotted a small, auburn-haired figure in the passenger seat and recognized Dee. She raised her hand and waved. Dee didn't wave back. Through the car window Harley could tell that Dee was frowning.

Harley took that as a very bad sign. Even when they had been chased by deranged killers, Dee usually wore a grin. For Dee to be frowning, something had to be terribly wrong. Harley only hoped Dee hadn't told her father about the dead man. Otherwise it was going to be a very unpleasant morning.

The blue-and-white police car pulled into the circle drive in front of the big house and crunched to a stop. The driver's-side door opened, and Chief Janes stepped out. The chief was dressed in his police uniform, with a dark blue jacket and crisp khaki trousers. The wooden handle of a heavy revolver jutted from a leather holster on his waist, and handcuffs hung down against his hip. Mirrored sunglasses covered his eyes, but there was no hiding the grim expression on his face.

"Hi," Harley called uncertainly. She worked up a smile. "What are you guys doing out here?"

"I'm here because we need to talk," replied Chief Janes. The tone of his voice was hard and low. It wasn't the voice of the man who had taken Harley in when her father disappeared—it was the no-nonsense voice of Stone Harbor's chief of police.

Harley nodded in reply. "All right," she said. "What do we talk about?"

Chief Janes glanced over at the car, where his daughter was sitting. Even through the silver lenses of his sunglasses, Harley caught some of the angry fire in his look.

13

"You are never to see my daughter again. Is that clear?"

Harley felt as if she had been kicked in the chest. Dee was her best friend! "But—"

"No buts," Chief Janes said firmly. "This is an absolute condition. Are we clear?"

The police chief's words were so unexpected, Harley didn't know what to think. "No," she answered. "We're *not* clear. Why are you doing this?"

"Because I have to," Chief Janes replied. "Ever since you arrived in Stone Harbor, Dee has been disobeying my instructions and getting involved in situations that endanger her life." He shook his head. "I won't have any more of it."

The passenger door on the police car suddenly flew open. Dee leaped out with an expression of fury stamped across her round face. "You can't blame Harley for what I've done!" she shouted. "She didn't *make* me do anything!"

The police chief turned to face his daughter. He reached up and pushed his sunglasses onto his broad forehead. His eyes were as cold as the nearby Atlantic. "I know where the blame lies," he said, his voice filled with cold iron. "I thought I told you to stay in the car."

Dee shook her head. Standing beside her father and the big police car, Dee looked tiny. She was barely five feet tall, and her small, freckled features made her seem even younger than she was. But there was nothing small about Dee's anger. "I'm not going to sit in the car while you blame everything on Harley," she seethed at her father. "I *know* I didn't listen to you. I *know* I was in danger. But I *had* to do it."

"She saved my life," Harley added. "If Dee hadn't come to help me—"

Chief Janes cut her off with a sharp wave of his hand. "This isn't about who's right and who's wrong. It's not about *why.*" He let the mirrored glasses fall back across his eyes. "Get back in the car, Dee. Otherwise I may have to carry out my promise."

Dee scowled, and the skin between her eyes pinched into tight folds. "You mean your *threat?*" She glanced from her father to Harley. "All right. I'm going." Dee climbed back into the car and closed the door with a slam that shook the ground.

Harley stared after her in surprise. Dee had risked her father's anger a dozen times to help Harley or Noah. Nothing had convinced her to stay out of the game before. "What kind of threat did you make?" she asked.

"It's simple," replied the police chief. "I told Dee that if she got involved in this mess again, the FBI would suddenly get a very good lead in their search for the mysterious Harley Davisidaro."

Once again Harley felt almost flattened by surprise. "You'd turn me in?" she gasped.

The police chief nodded sharply. "I don't want to do it, but I will if I have to."

Harley opened her mouth to reply, but before she could say anything, Kenyon emerged from the shrubs at the edge of the house. "There's no need for that," he said. "We've decided that Stone Harbor isn't the most secure site for future operations." Even with sand from the dead agent's grave still clinging to the cuffs of his pants, Kenyon sounded like he had just wandered out of some executive boardroom. He walked up to the edge of the driveway and stood facing the police officer. "We're leaving Stone Harbor right away."

The police chief turned toward Kenyon and nodded. "I can't say that I disagree with your decision," he replied. "You two have made plenty of enemies, and if you stay around here, they'll know exactly where to find you."

Harley felt a tightening in her stomach. She knew that Mr. Janes had been upset about Dee sneaking out to help them, but Harley hadn't thought he would be eager to see her move away—or turn her over to the authorities. "If that's what you want," she said slowly, "we can leave today."

"Good," Mr. Janes replied. "I think that would be for the best." He paused and glanced through the windshield at Dee. "For all of us."

Through the blue tinted glass along the top of the windshield, Harley thought she could see Dee crying. "We'll leave," Harley said softly.

The police chief's mirrored sunglasses glowed red in the evening light. "I'd like a word with Ms. Davisidaro in private," he told Kenyon.

Kenyon seemed to be considering some kind of response, but at last he only nodded. "I'll go inside and pack."

"You can wait here," said Chief Janes. "I need to take Ms. Davisidaro far enough away that my daughter can't listen in."

Harley shrugged. "All right." She turned and strode across the damp green lawn. She was careful to lead the chief away from the place where she and Kenyon had been burying the dead man. As angry as he was, the chief didn't seem to know anything about the dead body. Harley wanted to keep it that way. She walked around a screen of thick, tangled hedges and waited for the police officer to join her.

As soon as Chief Janes came around the hedge the expression on his face changed. The mask of stony indifference fell away, replaced by a look of concern. He reached up and pulled off his reflecting sunglasses. "Are you sure you're doing the right thing?" he asked.

"What?" Harley frowned.

"Leaving," said Mr. Janes. "Are you certain that's the right thing to do?"

Harley felt more confused than ever. "I thought you *wanted* me to go away."

Chief Janes shook his head. "*Want* has got nothing to do with this," he replied. "What I want most is for Dee to be safe, but don't run off and get yourself killed just because I'm worried." He paused and looked at Harley for a moment with his lips pressed into a tight line. "Do you have anywhere to go?" he asked at last.

Harley shrugged again. "Kenyon's family has some property near Chicago," she said. "We could head up there. But Unit 17 probably already knows about that place."

The police chief nodded. "It'll be hard to find somewhere that these secret organizations *don't* know about. It's clear that they have access to police and FBI records. They'll be watching for you."

"I know." Harley looked across the lawn toward the distant ocean. "We may have to run for a long time."

"I wish . . ." Chief Janes's voice trailed away, and he squeezed his eyes closed. "Harley, I wish it didn't have to be this way," he said in a choked voice. "I've been a policeman my whole adult life. I'm supposed to protect people. I wish I could tell you to come back and stay with us and graduate high school with Dee and live a normal life."

Harley shook her head slowly. "But you can't do that."

Mr. Janes opened his gray eyes. "No," he said quietly. "I can't." He reached into the pocket of his uniform trousers, pulled out a business card, and pressed it into Harley's hand. "Wherever you go, I want you to take this with you. It has my number at the police station and the number at home. If you need help, you can call me anytime—day or night."

Harley turned the little card over in her hands, then shoved it into the back pocket of her jeans. "We may be a long way from Stone Harbor."

"Don't worry," said Mr. Janes. "I may just be a small-town cop, but I have friends. If you need something, you call."

Part of the terrible weight that had been pressing down on Harley's heart began to lift slightly. She gave a brief smile. "I will," she said.

Chief Janes nodded quickly. His face settled back into firm, unemotional lines. He slid the mirrored sunglasses from his pocket and settled them back on his nose. "Now let's go out there and put on a good show for Dee," he said. "I don't want her to think this situation is anything but absolutely serious."

"Oh, I think Dee knows it's serious," said Harley.

They walked around the hedge and found Kenyon and Dee standing beside the car. When she saw her father, Dee held up her hands. "I know, I'm not supposed to get out of the car."

"Exactly," replied Chief Janes. "Get back in. We're leaving."

Dee planted her hands on her hips. "I'm going to say good-bye. You owe me that much."

"I don't owe you anything," her father replied. He paused and glanced over at Harley. "Say your good-byes. You've got one minute." He opened the car door, sat down, and closed the door behind him.

Dee hurried around the front of the car and hugged Harley. "Talk fast," she said. "Tell me how much you're going to miss me."

Harley laughed, but her vision swam with the beginning of tears. "I *am* going to miss you. I think I'd have gone nuts by now if it wasn't for you."

"Naw," said Dee. "You wouldn't go nuts."

"I wouldn't?"

Dee shook her head. "Without me you'd be dead." She gave Harley another hug, then backed away. She turned and waggled her finger at Kenyon. "You take good care of her."

Kenyon nodded. "We'll be careful."

"You better." Dee rushed to him and threw her arms around him.

For a moment Harley thought Kenyon was going to pull away—healthy shows of emotion weren't exactly his thing, and Dee and Kenyon hadn't always gotten along like the best of friends. But to Harley's surprise Kenyon put his hands on Dee's waist, lifted her off the ground, and planted a kiss on her cheek. "You watch out," he warned her. "Just because we're gone doesn't mean the goon squad is going to vacate Stone Harbor overnight."

Dee clung to him for a moment, then pulled away.

"I don't suppose either one of you has heard anything from Scott?"

"No," Kenyon replied. "Not yet."

Dee nodded. "I . . . I'm sure he's all right." She looked down at her feet.

Harley bit her lip. Dee and Scott had been together since the first moment they met, and their relationship had seemed to be one of the few bright spots among the shadows. But when Scott's long lost friend Chloe appeared, Scott had followed her out of town, leaving Dee behind. "If we hear from him, we'll call you," Harley promised. "Okay?"

Dee nodded again. She wiped tears away from her brown eyes with the back of her hand. Dee smiled weakly and then briskly walked around to the side of the police car. "See you around, right?"

"Absolutely," replied Harley. "This craziness can't last forever."

Fresh tears rolled down Dee's cheeks. She pulled open the car door and slid inside. Immediately Chief Janes put the car in gear and looped around the circle drive. In a few seconds the police car was on its way back down the slope.

Kenyon stood beside Harley until the car reached the highway, then turned back toward the house. "Come on," he said. "We have a chore to finish."

"Yeah." As Harley followed him across the grass, she wasn't sure how she felt about the idea of leaving Stone Harbor for good. Terrible things had happened in and around the town, but it was also the place where she had met Dee . . . and Noah Templer. At one time she had hated the town, but now she actually thought she would miss it.

Harley was so caught up in thinking about leaving that she didn't notice Kenyon had stopped until she walked right into his back. She stumbled away from the collision and shook her head. "What's going on?"

"The body," said Kenyon. He pointed toward the shallow scar in the sand dunes where they had dug the grave.

Harley stepped around him and peered at the sandy ground. The heavy canvas tarpaulin they had used to wrap the body was there, but now it was unfolded and spread over the sand. Faint smudges of blood and dirt streaked the stiff cloth.

The body was gone.

TWO

Sunset came fast in the desert.

Scott Handleson pushed open a screen door at the back of a white clapboard building and stepped out onto the narrow wooden deck. Already the air was starting to lose some of the blazing dry heat of midday. He rubbed his tired eyes, walked over to the side of the deck, and leaned against the sturdy railing.

If the sun was already setting over the badlands, it was dark back in Stone Harbor. Dee might be studying for school, or watching television, or sleeping. Scott stared out across the dry, barren land. One thing was sure, with the way he had run away from Dee, she probably wasn't thinking about him. Or if she was, Scott doubted she was thinking anything very nice.

Ever since they first met, Dee and Scott had been a couple. Scott had never known anyone as funny—and as fun—as Dee. She was smart, and brave, and a whole lot prettier than she thought she was. Sometimes it seemed to Scott that he had spent his whole life running from place to place, barely even noticing the people around him. Dee had changed that. She had made him feel more comfortable than he had at any time in his life. But he had thrown Dee over in a second when he found Chloe.

Scott closed his eyes and clenched the wooden rail. He had spent more than five years searching for

Chloe. Then, just when he had almost given up, Chloe had found him. But the reunion hadn't been as happy as Scott had dreamed. Chloe had arrived in Stone Harbor with warnings that one of the secret organizations was closing in. It had come down to a choice: stay in Stone Harbor to help Dee and his friends or leave with Chloe.

Scott had chosen Chloe. Only hours after she had come, he was on his way out of town, leaving Dee, Kenyon, and Harley behind.

I had to do it, he thought. I looked for her so long, I couldn't risk losing her again. It was the truth, but it didn't stop Scott from wondering if he had made the right decision. And it didn't reduce the guilt he felt about the way he had left Stone Harbor.

He opened his eyes and looked around the compound. The long, low buildings of the Daystar Cooperative lay against the desert hardpan like a pack of resting dogs. Surrounding the buildings was a wide swath of dry, yellowed fields and bare stony ground broken by stands of prairie grass and stunted juniper trees. In one of the nearest fields Scott spied a tight cluster of cooperative members still working in the growing darkness. They hoed at the hard ground with such frantic energy that Scott almost expected to see sparks flying from their tools. In their crisp new jeans and pale green polo shirts, Scott thought the Daystar people had to be some of the best-dressed farmers in the state. Except they weren't really farmers.

Despite the clean, boring appearance of the place, everything about the compound gave Scott the creeps.

The cooperative looked normal only because it had been carefully *designed* to look normal. The clean-cut, hardworking image had been planned to every square window and flat white wall. The signs at the edges of the property explained how the cooperative was designed to draw on the best elements of a sixties commune and an Israeli kibbutz. The dry fields didn't show much production, but anyone in the surrounding communities was sure to say good things about the place. The Daystar workers paid their bills on time. They kept the place neat. And they caused no trouble. They seemed like perfect neighbors.

Scott could have told a different story. The Daystar workers were a long way from being a group of idealistic farmers trying to keep up a little place on the edge of the badlands. The whole Daystar compound was nothing but the latest cover for a group that had been in existence for as long as history had been recorded. Except for Scott, every single person at the compound was a member of the secret organization called Umbra.

The screen door squeaked behind him, and soft footsteps sounded on the boards of the deck. "There you are," said a voice.

He turned to see Chloe Adair smiling at him. The fading light painted her honey blond hair with darker tones and left shadows over the curves of her face. For a moment Scott flashed on the image of a younger Chloe—the small girl he had known at the orphanage where they had both grown up. But as she stepped closer, that image shattered. The orphanage was more than five years in the past, and Chloe Adair was no

24

longer a mischievous girl with a mass of short curls and a daredevil grin. Chloe had grown into the most beautiful woman Scott had ever seen.

If she had been ugly, he thought, would I have followed her halfway across the continent? The thought brought a fresh ripple of guilt. Scott didn't want to believe he had come with Chloe just because of the way she looked, but he couldn't deny that her beauty left him feeling dizzy.

Chloe walked up beside Scott and drew in a deep breath of the night air. "It's wonderful out here, don't you think?"

Looking at Chloe, Scott was inclined to agree. Wherever she was, it had to be wonderful. A warm, dry breeze blew up off the badlands and sent her long, wavy hair flying back. When they were kids, Chloe had been Scott's closest friend. He had thought of her as his only family. But since she had reappeared, Scott didn't know how to feel. One thing was sure—she didn't seem like his kid sister.

"I love this time of evening," said Chloe. She held up her arms and arched her back as she drew in another deep breath. "If only it didn't get so hot during the day."

The fluid grace of her movements nearly hypnotized Scott. "Um, I mean . . . um," he said, stumbling to respond. "Yeah. It gets hot."

Chloe glanced toward him. Even in the dim light her eyes sparkled. For a moment Scott could only look at her. It wasn't just that Chloe was attractive. There was a quality in everything she did that he had never seen in anyone else—a feeling of calmness. She was barely eighteen, a full year younger than Scott, but she seemed so much older and wiser.

Chloe closed her eyes and ran her fingertips lightly across the rough cedar boards of the railing. "It's cooling off nicely," she said. "It'll be just right for the ceremony tonight."

A chill wind seemed to blow over Scott's skin that had nothing to do with the cooling air. The members of the Daystar Cooperative might seem fairly normal— even boring—during the day. But Scott didn't think the other people in the area would think they were such good neighbors if they could visit the place at night.

"You're going to try the ceremony again tonight?" he asked.

Chloe nodded. "We've been so close the last few times," she said. "If we could just get a little extra energy into the circle—" She broke off and turned toward Scott. "I want you to join us."

Scott looked at her in surprise. "Me?" He shook his head quickly. For the two days he had been at the compound, he had kept as far away from the ceremonies as he could. Even from a distance he didn't like what he saw. "I don't think—"

"We need you," Chloe interjected. She reached out and took hold of both his hands. "You may be the only one who can put us over the limit of the energy requirements."

"But I don't know a thing about these ceremonies," Scott protested. "I don't even think I want to know."

Chloe smiled. Her even, white teeth shone in the twilight. "You don't have to," she said. "We know what we're doing. We just need your help."

Scott frowned. Chloe's fingers were warm and smooth against his hands, but he still felt cold when he thought about the ceremonies. "How can I help? I don't even believe in this stuff."

Chloe actually laughed. "Of course you do," she said. She gave his hands a last squeeze and then let them go. "We're not talking about some crazy mumbo jumbo. There are no chicken bones and shrunken heads."

The words pulled a smile from Scott. "I know—it's just not what I'm used to."

"Sure, it is," Chloe replied. "This is *science*, Scott. You proved that yourself."

"What do you mean?"

"Your machine." Chloe gestured toward the dark eastern sky. "Didn't that gizmo you built back in Stone Harbor measure the kind of energy we produce in the circle?"

Scott nodded slowly. "Yeah. I guess it could. At least it measures some kind of mental energy."

"If the energy can be measured with a machine, then it's no different than light or sound." Chloe pressed her lips together for a moment, then smiled again. "I know," she said. "It's like radio. People can't see radio waves passing through the air. They can't taste them or hear them. They only know that radio waves exist because they have a machine that can turn them into something they can hear."

"But radio waves don't come from the inside of people," Scott replied.

Chloe gave an exasperated sigh. "Now you're just

trying to be difficult," she said. She studied Scott's face. "You said that you spent five years searching for me. Now that we're together again, won't you help me?"

Scott winced. Even when they were kids, it had been hard to refuse her. "All right," he said softly. "I'll come, but I don't know what good it will do."

Instantly Chloe's smile cut through the darkness. "Thank you!" She leaned forward and kissed Scott on the cheek. "This will make the difference, you'll see."

A warm blush spread over Scott's face as he nodded. "I hope you're right," he said, but in his heart he wasn't sure that was true. He wondered what would happen if the ceremony was successful. From what Chloe had told him, the ceremony had to do with channeling the energy of the Umbra members to create the same kind of vortex that Unit 17 had created using tons of high-tech equipment—a white sphere. The sphere could act as a gateway to other worlds or as a transport to any point on Earth. It was incredibly powerful and horribly dangerous.

Like anything else, the sphere could be put to good use or to bad. "Why do you—"

But before Scott could finish his question, Chloe turned from him and waved to the workers in the field. "Come in!" she called. "It's time to prepare."

With the precision of soldiers lining up for a parade, the workers flipped their hoes onto their shoulders and walked toward the house. Scott felt another surge of uneasiness as he watched the Daystar workers put away their tools. The Umbra people looked like anyone else, but that didn't keep Scott from feeling that the whole crew was as creepy as midnight in a graveyard. Like the buildings of the compound, they were just *too* normal.

Chloe touched him on the arm. "Scott? Are you all right?"

"Yeah," he replied with a nod. "Yeah, I'm fine." He watched the last of the Daystar workers vanish into the buildings. Then he shrugged. "It's just hard for me to accept that you're really part of Umbra. I mean, I spent five years thinking that Umbra was holding you prisoner somewhere. I thought they were the bad guys."

Chloe's hand squeezed the muscles of his forearm. "Surely you've seen enough to know we're not like that."

Scott wasn't sure what to say. He still didn't trust Umbra. But even admitting that to himself made him feel guilty. Chloe was the head of Umbra. If he didn't trust Umbra, did that mean he didn't trust Chloe? "It's just going to take me some time," he said at last. "Give me a few days."

"I understand," said Chloe. Her fingers slid down to hold Scott's hand. An electric warmth spread over his skin at her touch. "Come with me tonight. It won't hurt. I promise." She raised her free hand and held up three fingers. "Scout's honor."

Scott tried to work up a smile. "All right."

"Good. Let's go get ready."

With his fingers still tangled in hers, Scott allowed Chloe to lead him into the building. The interior of the Daystar buildings was simple: white-painted walls and bare wood floors. The whole place was still new enough that it smelled of fresh paint, sawdust, and plaster. The rooms of the place were nearly bare, and the few pieces of furniture that were around looked like refugees from some army surplus store.

At least Scott was lucky enough to have a room to himself. Most of the Umbra members were packed into bunkhouses, with thirty or forty people all living in the same room. Too much of Scott's childhood had been spent in rooms like that. Since he had left the orphanage, he had always enjoyed having a bedroom of his own.

No one had bothered to turn on the lights in the central building, and Chloe led Scott down hallways that were clouded with gloom. Once again Scott flashed on an image of the younger Chloe. He remembered the way they had held hands as they walked through the dark tunnel that ran beneath the Benevolence Home. They had crept along the stone tunnels until they came to a chamber filled with chanting figures in dark purple robes. Then there had been shouting and robed figures moving through the shadows, and Chloe had been lost. Walking through the dark passages of the house gave Scott a feeling of déjà vu so strong that he could almost smell the damp, musty odors of that subterranean tunnel. His heart raced, and he felt goose bumps rise on his skin.

Don't be an idiot, he scolded himself. You're not a little kid, and this isn't the orphanage. He shook his head and threw off the memories that had gathered around him like cobwebs.

Instead of directing Scott to his own room, Chloe pulled him down a hallway to the door of a large empty chamber. Scott blinked and squinted into the darkness. "What's in there?"

"Just what we need to get ready." Chloe released his hand and stepped into the room. Then she reached to the back of her cotton dress, released the clasp, and let the soft garment slide to the floor.

Scott stared in amazement. "What are we doing?"

Chloe gave a soft laugh. "We're getting ready for the ceremony," she replied. She kicked away her shoes and padded across the room on bare feet.

Both confused and excited, Scott stepped into the room after her. Chloe's body was a pale form against the gloom. As Scott watched she opened a tall wooden closet at the end of the room and drew something from the shelves. "Catch!" she called, then she turned and tossed a dark shape toward Scott.

Scott let out a sharp breath and stepped back in alarm. The object fell on the floor at his feet with a soft thump.

Chloe laughed again. "You better pick that up," she said. "It'll get dusty."

Still unsure of what was going on, Scott knelt and reached out for the dark thing on the floor. His fingers closed on smooth, satiny cloth. "What is this?" he asked.

"It's a robe."

There was the sound of rustling cloth from across the room. When Scott looked up, he saw that Chloe's pale figure had disappeared into a spot of darkness. Once again he shivered as a memory swam up from the past. "Do we have to wear this?" Scott asked.

Chloe walked toward him. She had pulled the cowl of the robe over her head, and Scott could barely see the pale oval of her face inside the shadows of the hood. "Put on your robe," she said.

Scott picked up the garment from the floor and held it out in front of him. In the darkness the purple cloth looked almost black. "If this ceremony is based on science, then it won't matter what we wear."

Chloe sighed. "Wearing the robe won't hurt you," she explained. "It's traditional. Come on. Put it on and we can get going."

Reluctantly Scott slipped the robe on over his clothes and followed Chloe back through the dark building. The cloth fluttered around his legs as he walked, and the long loose sleeves swallowed his arms and hands. The hood of the robe did strange things to sound, filling Scott's ears with whispers.

After the darkness inside, the desert night seemed almost as bright as day. The sky overhead was filled with an incredible number of stars—so many that they cast a fuzzy shadow around Scott's feet as he followed Chloe down the steps and across the compound. The other members of Umbra were already emerging from the cluster of buildings. They streamed out the doors in their dark robes and joined Chloe and Scott as they walked toward the ceremony site.

The walk was eerily quiet. In a group this large, Scott would have expected to hear laughing, talking, whistling, even arguing, but there was none of that. The only sound was the movement of feet and the soft whisper of the robes against the dusty ground.

By the time they reached the ceremony site, Scott was feeling nervous again. The site was a flat sandy area trapped at the end of a small box canyon. Walls of reddish stone rose on three sides to block the view of the night sky. More stones had been used to form a rough circle on the ground. At the center of the circle a small fire licked at chunks of dry pine and cedar that popped and spit sparks into the night.

As the participants in the ceremony filed into the canyon, the fire threw twisted, jittering shadows against the stones. Scott felt completely out of place amid the hooded and robed figures. He wondered what Dee would say if she could see him now. Or Harley. He didn't have to wonder much about Kenyon. If Kenyon knew that Scott was taking part in a ceremony run by one of the secret groups, he would have been disgusted.

Chloe pulled Scott to the side of the circle. "Stay here," she whispered softly. Then she started to step away.

"Where are you going?" Scott whispered back.

She raised one voluminous sleeve of the robe and pointed toward the small fire. "It's my job to lead the ceremony tonight. Don't worry. Just stay right here."

Scott nodded. "But what do I do?"

"You'll know when the time comes," Chloe replied. She turned away and walked to the center of the circle.

The last of the Umbra members fell into place. Chloe stood near the small fire with her arms outstretched. Her black shadow spread over the sands like the image of some huge raven.

"Begin," she said. Her voice was soft, but it carried through the box canyon as loud as any shout.

At once the Umbra members began to sing a single,

wordless note. It was a deep tone, so low and rumbling that Scott not only heard it, he could feel it in the pit of his stomach. He swallowed nervously. Chloe was circling slowly around the flames, raising and lowering her arms. The circle of robed figures changed their note, moving up an octave. The new tone crawled over Scott's skin like a host of invisible ants.

What am I doing here? he wondered. I should leave. Chloe will be disappointed, but she'll understand.

Across the circle a woman suddenly raised her voice in a tone slightly higher than the one sung by the rest of the circle. On Scott's right a man lowered his voice by an eighth. To his left a second woman dropped deeper. One by one the members of the circle departed from the central note, each of them taking up a frequency all their own.

Then they began to sing.

It should have been chaos. It was chaos. But it was a beautiful chaos.

All around Scott a hundred voices were raised in a hundred different melodies, a hundred different keys, a hundred different rhythms. The voices crossed over each other, forming momentary harmonies, then broke apart. Some voices soared upward while others plunged into notes so deep they seemed impossible. Then from the center of the circle a new voice sounded.

Scott was transfixed. He couldn't move. He couldn't even draw a breath.

The new singer didn't have the loudest voice in the circle, or the highest, or even the strongest, but her notes cut through the rest of the songs like the beam of a lighthouse slicing through fog. Chloe stood with her arms slung out and her head thrown back. Light from the small fire penetrated the shadows of her robe and gleamed from her golden hair. Her song had no words, and the melody was unlike anything that Scott had ever heard. Her voice darted at notes like a hummingbird. It slid from one emotion to the next. Around her people moaned, and laughed, and shrieked—and it was all music.

All at once Scott found both his nervousness and his paralysis gone. It seemed to him that a sheet of music had appeared in his head. He could see the notes of the impossibly complex score glowing in his mind. Scott hadn't sung in public since he had escaped the choir at the orphanage. He hated to sing. He rarely even listened to the radio. But the music in his head wouldn't go away. It was bright, and pulsing, and powerful, and it demanded to be sung. Scott opened his mouth, threw back his head, and hurled the notes into the night sky.

His mind seemed to leave his body, traveling with the notes. He saw himself standing in the purple robe with red flashes of firelight chasing themselves across the glossy cloth. He saw Chloe in the center of the circle, her body trembling and shaking with her song. Around her the other members of Umbra began to jump and shuffle and sway as their songs drove them into an erratic, frantic dance.

I should be dancing, thought Scott. I should be dancing, too. He looked down at his own body, and he saw that he *was* dancing. His feet slid and hopped

35

beneath the fabric of the robe. His arms flailed, and his head rolled on his neck.

For a moment he tried to make sense of what was going on. He tried to make the clashing music and the jerky, writhing dance fit into some larger picture. He looked for the order and sense that he found in his science and math. But there was no picture. The songs and the dance made no sense. They weren't supposed to make sense. They weren't supposed to fit together or obey any rules.

It felt wonderful.

A powerful gust of cold wind bolted through the canyon. The small fire flared and fluttered in the breeze. In the space above Chloe a white mist was gathering. It was thin at first, like the steam over a pond on a cold morning, but it rapidly grew thicker. It revolved above Chloe, forming a cottony white ball.

It's happening, thought Scott. A sharp, keen excitement shook through his body. The door. The key. The words formed in his head as clearly as the notes of music.

The white ball spun faster and shrank still more. It began to glow with its own internal light. It was forming a white sphere.

All around the circle the tuneless songs gave way to screams and streams of meaningless words. Some people threw themselves to the sand. Others ripped at their robes. The pounding music in Scott's skull ended without warning. He drew a fresh breath, opened his mouth, and spilled out a gout of words.

"Iehal! Aaya, ua ualha!" he shouted. *"Ilya! Ilya!"* The words were nonsense, except . . . they weren't.

The words brought with them a host of twisting, changing images that seemed to spill from Scott's mind into the dark air around him. Bloodred. Midnight black.

The white sphere hung in the air above Chloe's head. It was small, no bigger than a golf ball, but it was impossibly bright.

Looking at it, Scott felt a feeling of ecstasy more intense than anything he had ever experienced in his life. They're coming, he thought. Now they will come.

Then there was a crack of thunder and the white sphere collapsed.

Scott was knocked off his feet as the implosion echoed through the canyon. He struck his head against the hard earth, and for a moment he saw nothing but the stars inside his own skull. His stomach surged. He lay on the cold sand, waiting for his mind to clear.

When he finally felt well enough to stand, he found Chloe peering down at him. She had thrown back her hood, and her wavy gold hair spilled onto her shoulders. She looked tired, but she didn't seem to be hurt. "Are you all right?" she asked.

Scott nodded carefully, trying not to upset his aching skull. The painfully strong excitement he had felt a few moments before was melting into confusion and disappointment. "I think so. What happened?"

Chloe smiled. "We had it," she said. "For a moment we really had it. The energy you added to the group made a difference."

"But not enough," Scott replied.

"Not quite." Chloe shook her head. "But we're

close. We're really close." She reached out and helped Scott to his feet. "I was right, wasn't I? No one had to tell you what to do."

Scott remembered the bright notes of alien music running through his head and smiled weakly. "No," he said. "I guess not." He tried to take a step, but he suddenly shivered so hard, it almost knocked him off his feet.

Chloe reached out to steady him. "Are you sure you're all right?"

"Yeah." Scott put his hands together and rubbed them as fast as he could. "It's just that all of a sudden, I feel really, really cold."

Harley ran the beam of her flashlight across the gray, sandy ground. "This is useless," she said. "That man was dead."

Kenyon stepped past her and directed his own light into the rolling field of sand dunes. He held the flashlight in his left hand and a large black pistol in his right. "I know he was dead, but the tracks around the grave showed someone walking this way."

"Since when did you become a frontier scout?" asked Harley. Hours of scouring the sandy ground for any trace of the dead man had left her tired and irritated.

"I know footprints when I see them." Kenyon paused beside a clump of saw grass and shone his light straight down. "Here. Take a look at this."

Harley sighed and walked over to take a look. A pair of footprints were pressed deep into the tan sand. One held the clear tread of a work shoe or boot. The other print was distorted and smeared to the side, as if whoever had made the print had staggered or limped. She tried to think of what kind of shoes the dead man had been wearing, but she hadn't paid much attention to his feet. "Are you sure *you* didn't make these?"

Kenyon held up his foot, revealing the smooth pattern on the bottom of his leather deck shoes. "Not mine."

"And they're not from some tourist looking for the perfect place to have a picnic?"

"We're four miles north of the public beach and almost half a mile from the water. They'd have to be desperate for that picnic."

Harley nodded reluctantly. She was anxious to get on the road and away from the madness in Stone Harbor, but leaving a dead man walking around seemed like a very bad idea. "All right, we keep looking."

They spent some time roaming over the dunes in search of more footprints, but the sand was dry and the wind was blowing stiffly in from the sea. If there had been any other footprints in the area, the shifting sand dunes had erased all signs. Finally Kenyon climbed higher into the dune field while Harley turned down toward the sea.

The sound of the surf hissed along the beach on Harley's right, growing louder with every step. As she came closer to the water, the dunes gradually flattened out to curving lines of driftwood and debris that marked the limit of high tide. Pale gray ghost crabs scuttled around Harley's feet.

Harley shivered. The wind off the sea was cold, but that wasn't the reason she was shaking. The darkness, the odd jerky movements of the crabs, and the thought that she was chasing a dead guy through the night all combined to give her a heavy-duty set of the creeps.

She turned up the slope to rejoin Kenyon, but as she moved, her flashlight picked up a series of tracks in the sand. Cautiously she stepped closer and shone the light straight down into the deep depressions in the sand. The tracks bore the same deep treads as the pair she had seen before. Once again one of the feet— the right foot—seemed to be dragging.

Harley raised her flashlight and shone the beam up the beach. The tracks continued. "Kenyon!" she shouted. "I think I found something!"

She heard a faint reply, but the wind off the sea swallowed the words and garbled them. Harley fixed her light on the line of tracks and followed them along the beach. The dead man—if the tracks did belong to him—seemed to be limping slowly closer to the water. In places the line of tracks had been erased by the waves, and shimmering foam filled the edges of other prints, but the direction of the tracks was clear enough.

"Kenyon!" Harley shouted again. "Come down here! Hurry!" She leaned down low and kept the light on the ground as she shuffled forward. The tracks moved through a puddle past a heap of wave-polished driftwood and disappeared over a rough patch of bare rock. They picked up on the other side of the stone, crossed a yard of clean sand . . . and ended in a pair of boots.

Harley felt a sudden terror that squeezed her so tight, she couldn't have screamed to save her life. With a trembling hand she raised the flashlight. The cone of light drifted across a pair of trousers that were stained by grass and grave dirt, up over a shirt with ragged holes and brown splotches of dried blood, and onto a gray, dead face.

The dead man stood with his head tilted to the side at such a sharp angle that it nearly rested on his right shoulder. His mouth hung open, and the tip of his swollen, pale tongue jutted between his teeth. Grains of sand from Harley and Kenyon's attempt at burial still clung to the skin of the man's face. His eyes were a milky blue—as cold and empty as a mackerel under plastic wrap at the grocery store.

Harley's legs, which were normally capable of carrying her through a ten-mile run, seemed to turn to liquid. She stumbled back in ragged boneless steps, keeping the beam of her flashlight fixed on the dead man's face. She tried to call for Kenyon, but all that came out of her mouth was a low, dry sob.

Something shifted below the skin of the dead man's face. As Harley watched in horror, one of the lifeless eyes bulged from its socket. A silver snake slipped out of the gap in the corner of the eye. The snake was no bigger around than a strand of spaghetti, with two pinpoint black eyes at one end. Its head pulled a few inches out from the man's face, swung back and forth through the air for a moment, then snapped back like a rubber band.

"What . . . ," breathed Harley. "What are you?"

For a dead man the thing was surprisingly fast. The zombie struck Harley an underhanded blow that caught her on the chin and sent her spinning backward. Her heel caught against the patch of stone and she sat down hard enough that her teeth clacked together. The flashlight flew from her hand and spun into the water. A fresh wave crashed down, and for a moment the beach was lit with an eerie green-tinted light.

The zombie limped toward her. With its outstretched hands and dragging foot, it looked like a refugee from some late night movie—the kind of movie where everyone died.

Harley wasn't waiting to see how the movie turned out. She reached to her left and grabbed a length of driftwood from the sand. The branch was a good five feet long and only a little bigger around than her thumb. It had been worn bone white by sea and sun. The sand-crusted wood wasn't only bone colored, it was bone hard.

Harley waved it at the zombie. "Stay back, Igor," she warned. "I don't want to—"

The zombie rumbled deep in its chest and rushed at her awkwardly. Harley rose on one knee and drove the shaft of wood into the creature's guts. The drift-wood sank in with sickening ease. Thick black fluid gushed from the wound and spilled over Harley's hands as the wood drove through the thing's stomach, glanced from its spine, and ripped through its shirt to emerge from its back.

Harley let go of the wood with a cry of disgust. The fluid from the zombie was thick, sticky, and horribly cold. She rolled away and splashed into cold water at the ocean's edge.

The creature paused. Its face was slack and unchanging, but the tall body swayed unsteadily. The thing stood up straight, then reached clumsily behind its back. Gray fingers fumbled at the wood, got a grip, and pulled. In three sharp jerks the length of drift-wood slid completely through the zombie's midsection. The dead fingers opened, and the gore-soaked wood dropped to the beach.

Harley's stomach tightened in a convulsion of disgust. "Stay back!" she shouted. She tried to sound tough, but the words came out in something close to a scream. "Stay away from me!" She looked around her for some new weapon.

There was no time. The zombie put on an unexpected burst of speed. It reached Harley in two jerky strides, slipped cold fingers around her neck, and lifted her from the ground.

Harley raised her arms and beat at the dead thing's chest. Her fists drummed against its ribs with a hollow sound. Fresh gouts of black fluid spilled from the opening in its stomach. The zombie's fingers dug into Harley's flesh, cutting off all air.

Harley clawed at the creature's slack face. The skin pulled away with horrifying ease, exposing raw, red muscle. The torn skin dangled in a loose, ragged flap. For a fraction of a second Harley saw a half dozen of the silver snakes staring at her through the tear in the zombie's skin, then they slithered away to safety deeper in the dead flesh.

A gray fog gathered across Harley's vision, and black spots followed. She could hear her own blocked blood pounding in her throat as the dead man stared into her face with flat, lifeless eyes.

A gunshot cut through the night, and the zombie staggered to the side. The expression on the torn, dead face didn't change. A second shot followed the first. This time the creature released its grip.

Harley fell to the ground and gasped for breath. Her throat felt bruised, and every sip of air burned like fire—but it was the sweetest fire she had ever known. She had a vague sense of motion on the beach—someone running, another gunshot, a heavy thud.

Then Kenyon was leaning over her. "Are you all right?" he demanded.

Harley nodded weakly. "I think so," she replied in a hoarse whisper. She raised her head and looked down the beach. The zombie was lying facedown in the sand a dozen yards away. It seemed to be missing an arm. "What did you do?"

"I shot it." Kenyon reached down and helped Harley to her feet. "I hit it with three fléchette bundles," he said. "Those things are like a bunch of needles all shoved into one bullet. One is enough to stop an elephant, but it took two before that thing even let you go."

Harley stared at the body. "There's something inside the zombie."

"What do you mean?"

"It's like . . . worms." Harley's stomach jumped toward her throat, and she wrinkled her nose in disgust. "It's full of little snakes that look like they're made out of wire."

"That's imposs—" started Kenyon, but before he could finish, the zombie began to get up.

Having only one arm seemed to give the thing quite a problem, but eventually it made it onto its knees and from there to its feet. It began to limp away down the beach. There was a hole in its chest so large that Harley could see the moonlit beach through the gap.

"Hold it there!" screamed Kenyon.

To Harley's surprise, the zombie actually stopped. With slow and jerky movements it turned. The face was covered in silver snakes. The small snake heads jutted from the mouth and eyes and from the tears in the skin where Harley had fought for her life. They bobbed and swayed in the air like a nest of vipers.

Harley felt as if she was going to lose every bite of food she had eaten in the last year. She turned away from the thing's horrible, ripped face. "Shoot it again," she told Kenyon. "Watch out—it's faster than it looks."

"Right." Kenyon raised his big semiautomatic pistol.

The zombie gave out a rough rattling sigh, then an eerie voice floated along the beach. "Waahhhh . . . wait. Donnnnn . . . don't shoot."

"What are you?" she breathed.

"Thaaa . . . that is not your concern," said the voice. The dead man's mouth didn't move, but Harley knew that the words emerged from that rotting throat. "This . . . this unit is . . . is in transit. Leeee . . . leave it alone and no . . . harm will come to any of you."

Kenyon shook his head. "That's not good enough," he said. "Here's the deal. You tell us what's going on, or I'll blow your 'unit' into a thousand pieces."

The dead man didn't respond.

"You've got three seconds to think about it," Kenyon continued. He straightened his arm and sighted carefully along the top of the pistol. "One—"

"Alllll . . . all right," moaned the distant voice. "Do not cause furrrrr . . . further harm to the unit. What information do you desire?"

Harley spoke first. "What are you?" she asked. "Who do you work for?"

There was a brief pause, then the zombie shifted slightly to the side. "This unit was formerly a memmm . . . member of the organization called

46

Legion. It is being taken to the correct site for collection."

Legion. Harley knew that the organization was involved in breeding people for some purpose. Noah Templer was supposed to be a product of Legion's vast and monstrous experiment. Harley had seen one of Legion's agents who had been assigned to watch over Noah, and she had encountered the floating red spheres that they generated from some unknown process. But she really knew very little about what the organization was like.

Kenyon waved his gun toward the zombie. "But that body's dead," he said sharply. "How is it moving?"

Again there was a pause. Harley was about to suggest that Kenyon restate his threat when the scratchy voice spoke again. "Previous to d-d-d . . . death, this agent was infected with genetically enhanced parasitic organisms. On death these ooo . . . organisms replicated and animated his form."

Harley felt her stomach give another lurch. "You mean it's those snake things that are making the body move?"

"Yes," said the voice. "They also provide an interface for remote operation and exude a chemical that preserves brain tissue. If we can reee . . . recover the unit without further damage, we may be able to perform salvage."

Harley looked at the tattered body with its missing arm and gaping hole in the chest. "You mean you could bring him back to life?"

"Nnnnoooo. We would salvage. The body is lost. Only the *kah-em* will survive."

The word meant nothing to Harley, but she wasn't sure she really wanted to understand. Considering what she had already seen of Legion's technology, she hated to think what they would do with their dead agent once they got him home.

Kenyon took a step toward the zombie. "Why was this man at my house?" he asked. "Did you send him to kill me or Harley?"

The cluster of tiny snakes swung to face him. "We didn't www . . . want to kill anyone," said the voice. "We came here to retrieve our prrr . . . property."

"What property?"

"Chloe Adair and Scott Handleson."

Harley jerked with shock. "Scott and Chloe are part of your program? Like Noah?"

The dead man's head jerked stiffly. "I can't provide any mmmm . . . more information in this area." The cluster of snakes moved with increased activity, then withdrew into the dead flesh. "This unit is approaching the eee . . . end of its preservation period. It must continue to the retrieval point or we will begin to lose engrams."

"Too bad," said Kenyon. "What happened to Scott and Chloe? Did you take them?"

"Our operative was killed," said the voice. "We have no information on what happened to our property."

A snarl twisted Kenyon's features. "Scott's a *person*," he spat out. "I don't care what you had to do with his being born—he's *not* your property."

"This unit must return," said the voice.

The gun fired with a thunderous blast and a flash that left Harley dazzled. A fountain of sand rose from the ground beside the zombie.

"You leave when I say," barked Kenyon. "Who killed your agent?"

A single snake poked from the dead man's mouth and waved in the air. "Www . . . we don't know. We may obtain this information through salvage."

Kenyon glanced over at Harley. "I don't think we're going to learn any more. I think I should finish it."

"Wait." Harley looked at the terrible figure of the zombie. "If we let you salvage," she called, "will you learn anything about what happened to Scott and Chloe?"

"We cannot know the answer until we salvage," came the rattling reply.

"If you learn something about them when you salvage," said Harley, "will you share that information with us?"

After a short pause the dead man's head nodded jerkily. "Wwwww . . . we will share."

Harley turned to face Kenyon. "We thought Scott and Chloe left on their own, but whoever killed this Legion agent might have taken them."

"We don't know that."

"Exactly," Harley replied with a nod. "This is our best chance to find out."

"What makes you think there's any chance at all?" Kenyon asked. He gestured toward the zombie with his black pistol. "If we let this thing go, it might carry information about *us* back to Legion. There's no reason to believe we'll ever hear from them again."

"What information about us is there?" asked Harley. "Legion already knew how to find us. What other secrets do we have?"

Kenyon scowled. "If we let you have your salvage, why should you keep your word?"

"The word of Legion has been good through twenty centuries," replied the voice. "It is g-g-g . . . good today."

Kenyon made a growling noise deep in his throat, but he gradually lowered his gun. "All right," he said. "I'll let it live—if you can call this living."

Harley nodded. "If you learn anything," she called to the dead agent, "send the information to the chief of police in Stone Harbor."

"We will send the information." The zombie shifted on its feet. Somewhere in the dead body there was a cracking sound followed by a sickening gurgle. "This unit must leave now, or there will be no salvage. The *kah-em* is endangered."

"Go," said Kenyon. "Get away before I change my mind."

The zombie pivoted on stiff legs and lurched away into the night.

Scott tipped the metal bucket and poured out water onto the hot, dry ground. The desert soil drank up the water as fast as he poured, leaving only a circle of dampness on the hard earth.

All around Scott the members of the Daystar Cooperative hoed at the ground, and planted seed corn, and cleared the larger rocks from the field. They talked quietly among themselves as they worked, and several times a ripple of laughter passed through the fields as one of the workers called out a joke. Scott didn't know what to think. He had spent five years thinking of Umbra as an organization made up of trolls, and goblins, and vampires. But the people around him seemed like normal men and women.

After what had happened at the ceremony, Scott wondered if he was also part of Umbra. He had never felt anything like the depths of emotion that had come over him in the wild dancing and singing. In the morning light, the whole situation seemed a little silly. The idea that he had been jumping around like a madman and yelling his lungs out in front of a bunch of strangers was embarrassing. Still, Scott knew that if he had a chance to join in the ceremony again, he would find it hard to resist.

An elderly woman with white hair tied back in a long braid approached Scott with a gleaming bucket in her arms. "You don't need to carry any more water this morning," she called as she came up. "I'm your replacement. The Ipolex wants to see you."

Scott frowned. "The what?"

The question drew a laugh from the woman. "The Ipolex," she repeated. "The leader of our cell."

"You mean Chloe?"

At the mention of Chloe's name, the woman glanced away. "Yes," she said. "The Ipolex has asked that you come as soon as it is convenient."

"Then I guess I'll go," said Scott.

He left the old woman standing in the field and walked past the rows of workers to reach the main building. There was no air-conditioning, but just getting out of the blazing sun made Scott feel a hundred percent cooler. He walked from room to room and found Chloe sitting on the floor of the room where they had changed clothes the night before.

To Scott's surprise, Chloe was dressed in her dark purple robe. She sat with her legs crossed. The cowl of the robe was pulled away from her head and lay in folds on her shoulders. In her arms she held a huge black book with rough leather binding and heavy brass buckles at the corners. Two other women, also dressed in the soft robes, sat on the floor, facing Chloe. One was a young girl of thirteen or fourteen. The other was older, in her thirties or forties.

Chloe looked up at Scott and smiled at once. "You're here. Good." She stood up and gestured to the other women. "Leave now," she told them. "I will talk to you later." At once the two women stood, gave rapid bows, and padded out of the room without a word.

Scott turned to watch them walk away down the hall. "It's strange," he said.

"What is?" Chloe asked.

"The way everyone listens to you." Scott shrugged. "There are a lot of people here who are older, but everyone does what you say."

"Umbra respects ability, not age." Chloe walked up and stood so close to Scott that the loose cloth of her robe brushed against his bare arms. "That's always been the way."

"Are you really that strong?" Scott asked. "What kind of ability do you have?"

Chloe only smiled. She walked back to the center of the room, sat, then patted the floor in front of her. "Sit down with me and talk."

Scott felt clumsy as he lowered himself to the ground. He couldn't manage to fold his long legs as neatly as Chloe and had to sit with his feet sticking out in front of him. "What's in the book?" he asked, nodding toward the thick volume.

Chloe lifted the book from the floor and rested it on her legs. "This is called the *Ul'alahran,*" she said in reverent tones. "It's one of the ancient books lost to the world during the Dark Ages. Umbra members saved a copy and preserved it." She unbuckled the brass clasps and opened the dusty tome.

Scott leaned forward and saw that the pages were covered with very fine letters in some alphabet he didn't recognize. The ink was an odd rusty color. Scott reached to the book, but before he could touch the cracked parchment pages, he felt another wave of cold run through his body. He pulled back and squinted at the strange letters. "Can you read this?"

"I'm still learning." Chloe closed the heavy book and set it aside. "Just because I've got some special abilities doesn't mean I can do *everything.*"

Scott grinned. "I'm glad to hear it. I thought you had turned into superwoman while I wasn't looking."

Chloe returned his grin with one of her own. "What about you?" she asked. "I hear you got up at dawn and started working in the fields."

Scott shrugged. "It seemed like the right thing to do," he said. "I'm going to be living here, I should help out with the work. Besides, after . . ." He faltered as he tried and failed to find words for the emotions that had overwhelmed him during the ceremony. "After last night I feel like I'm more a part of this place."

"That's wonderful." Chloe's grin turned into a wide smile. "I was hoping you would find a niche for yourself here. I really wouldn't want to be without you again." Abruptly she rocked forward on her knees and kissed Scott hard on the mouth. It was a fast kiss, but it carried enough heat to leave Scott blushing.

He cleared his throat. "I, um . . . I wouldn't want to leave you either."

Chloe nodded. "I'm glad to see you wanting to help, but if you really want to help, there's something we need that you would be perfect for."

"What?" Scott tried to concentrate on Chloe's words, but the sudden kiss had thrown his thoughts into turmoil.

"We're setting up a communications system. It's

supposed to be some sort of digital link that combines radio and the Internet."

The discussion of electronics cleared Scott's mind. "A packet-switching network?"

Chloe waved her hand through the air. "I don't know," she said. "I'm afraid Umbra has never been very good with technical things. Umbra has other goals. Will you help us with the communications center?"

"Sure." Scott climbed to his feet and stretched out a kink in his sore shoulders, thinking about the brain computer Gunter Rhinehardt had used to scan information at Kenyon's mansion. "I think maybe I can figure out how to keep Legion from reading your messages."

"That would be wonderful." Chloe stood and faced him. "It's so great to have you here with me."

Scott felt his cheeks reddening again. "Thanks. Um, I guess I better go see about that communications system."

"Good," said Chloe. "Come back tonight and we'll talk."

"Okay." Scott turned to leave, but as he was going out the door another thought came to him about Rhinehardt. Something the Legion agent had said had been bothering Scott for days. He paused in the doorway and looked back. "Chloe?"

She glanced up at him, her honey blond hair spilling over the folds of her deep purple robe. "What is it?"

"Legion. Do you really think they . . . *made* us?"

Chloe was slow to answer. At last she nodded. "I think it's possible," she said. "Legion had been at their breeding program for a long time. There are probably a lot of people who live their whole lives and don't even know they were part of the experiment."

That idea made Scott feel as if he had lived his life inside a test tube. He felt a touch of anger at the sheer nerve of Legion. "What do you think it means?" he asked.

"It doesn't mean anything," Chloe replied. She reached up and ran one hand through her wavy hair. "Even if Legion did make us, we're out of their control now. We're not robots."

Her words made Scott feel a little better. "Right," he said. "We can do what we want." He turned, walked out of the house, and started across the compound toward the rocky outcropping where a trio of Umbra members were working to raise a slender radio tower.

Inside the small building beside the tower, the Umbra members had boxes of equipment marked with the names of computer makers and electronics manufacturers. Several of the boxes were opened, but nothing was yet set up. In the corner of the room a man stood reading from a paper brochure.

"Hi," called Scott. "I was sent over here to help."

The man looked up. He appeared to be in his midtwenties. He had brown hair clipped in a short, stiff cut, and brown eyes set into an angular face. A thin, crinkled scar ran from the corner of his right eye up across his forehead. "You know anything about computers?" he asked.

Scott nodded. "I know a little," he answered modestly.

The man with the scar smiled. "Good," he said. "You're in charge." He held out the computer manual with his left hand and put out his right for Scott to shake. "My name's Drake."

It was the first time any of the Umbra members had really introduced themselves to Scott. He took the man's hand. "I'm Scott. Nice to meet you." Drake's handshake was firm and dry. "Let's see what we've got."

For the next few minutes Drake showed Scott the list of materials. None of the Umbra members at Daystar might have been a computer expert, but *someone* had done a good job of ordering equipment. "We've got everything here," Scott said as he scanned the list. "Packet radio, satellite uplink, even laser relays for a T3 connection in Rapid City." He put down the papers and shook his head in wonder. "This is impressive."

"We need good communications," said Drake. "Can you help us get this set up?"

Scott nodded. "We won't finish today, but by the end of the week we should have all the data links in place."

They went outside and joined the crew in putting up the radio tower. Then Scott spent the afternoon helping to assemble the satellite dish. By sunset the communications building was flanked by the two antennas and the computer equipment inside was beginning to take shape. Scott was sweating over the installation of a network hub when Drake walked up and clapped his hand against Scott's back.

"Come on," Drake said. "You've done a hard day's work. Now it's time."

Scott clicked a pair of connectors together and stood. "Time for what?"

"Time to get ready for the ceremony."

Only a day before, Scott had been frightened by the whole idea of the ceremony. The ring of figures in robes had reminded him of the caverns where he lost Chloe, and the chanting and movements had seemed dark and frightening. But after taking part in the ceremony only once, the idea of going again started Scott's heart pounding in anticipation.

He followed Drake out of the communications building and across the flat central square of the compound. A few Umbra members were still on their way in from the fields, but most had already gone inside to prepare. A few had even finished donning their robes and were walking toward the ceremony ground.

Drake peeled away and walked toward one of the long bunkhouses as Scott turned toward the building where Chloe had given him a room. As he walked, his mind swirled with thoughts of Chloe, the computer system, and the upcoming ceremony. He was so distracted that he ran straight into a tall, robed figure coming out of the house.

Scott bounced away from the robed form as if he had struck an iron wall. "Sorry," he said. "I wasn't looking where I was going."

The figure in the robe stood still for a moment, then nodded slowly. He turned and moved toward the ceremony site.

Scott stood and watched the tall shape walk away. He shook his head. *The light was bad,* he thought. *That's all it was. He had his hood up, and the light was bad.*

But his own reassurances did little to quiet the tight feeling of fear that gnawed at Scott's stomach. *It was a trick of the light,* he told himself again, and this time he almost believed it.

But for a moment Scott could have sworn that the figure in the robe had no face.

It felt great to be on a motorcycle again.

Harley twisted the throttle of the Sportster 880 and smiled as the bike raced along the dark street. She could almost convince herself that her whole stay in Stone Harbor had been nothing but a dream. There was no secret military organization called Unit 17. Her father had not vanished. And there were certainly no walking zombies filled with genetically designed worms. All that stuff was just part of some weird nightmare.

But it wasn't true. Her father really was gone. So was Noah, and so was almost everything that Harley had once thought of as normal. Even the motorcycle she was riding wasn't the original Sportster she had ridden into town. That bike had been stolen by Unit 17—just like they had stolen her life.

The radio in her helmet crackled. "Slow down," Kenyon's voice ordered through a burst of static. "You're getting too far ahead."

Harley glanced into her mirror and saw the tiny reflection of Kenyon's van. "You know where the beach house is," she replied. "You don't need me to lead you there."

"I can find the beach house," Kenyon said, an edge of impatience in his voice. "But we only escaped from Unit 17 a couple of days ago. Scott and Chloe are missing. There was a dead man in my yard. Do you really want to go in there alone and end up being captured or killed?"

"I see your point." Harley eased off on the throttle. She hated to admit that Kenyon was right, but being caught by Unit 17 hadn't exactly been her idea of fun. If slowing down on the bike was the cost of staying out of their reach, she was willing to slow. Besides, there would be plenty of time to open up the Sportster and let it rip if they drove all the way to Chicago.

The next curve in the road brought her down onto the low dunes near the beach. Glancing to her left, she could see the phosphorescent glow of waves breaking against the sand. The drive leading to the beach house came up quickly. Harley turned onto the rutted road and found herself heading directly toward the swollen moon. She could see the beach house sitting in the distance. The small building seemed dark, quiet, and unoccupied. There appeared to be no assassins, shadow men, or zombies waiting to kill the first visitor. But Harley knew very well that appearances could be deceiving. "I'm there," she called over the radio.

Kenyon's reply came quickly. "Don't go inside," he said in a firm tone.

Harley was a little irritated at the way Kenyon always acted as if he was giving orders. But in this case Harley was happy enough to obey. "I'm not going anywhere," she called back. "Hurry up."

She waited until the van had turned into the mouth of the drive before going closer to the beach house. For extra safety Harley stopped the bike fifty yards from the house and killed the engine. She was just taking off her helmet when Kenyon pulled up in the van.

Harley studied Kenyon as he hopped out and marched around to the front of the vehicle. Weeks of working out had broadened his shoulders and added muscle to his arms. His dark hair had been trimmed, but it was still shaggier than it had been when Harley first met him. In the few months they had known each other, Kenyon had come a long way from the snotty rich kid Harley had encountered in Washington, D.C.

Since Noah vanished into the white sphere, Harley had probably spent more time with Kenyon than she had with anyone else. They had traveled together and fought the secret organizations together. They had risked their lives for each other. But despite all the time they had spent and the danger they had shared, Harley didn't know how she felt about Kenyon.

When they decided to leave Stone Harbor, it seemed only natural that they should go together. But the more Harley thought about it, the less certain she was that going with Kenyon was right.

If it wasn't for Kenyon, Harley thought, I'd be alone. But is that enough of a reason to stay together? Sometimes she thought there might be more between them than just a mutual fear and hatred for the secret groups, but . . .

Kenyon's dark brows drew together. "What's wrong?" he asked.

"Nothing," said Harley with a quick shake of her head. She glanced away, embarrassed by her thoughts. "Just thinking."

"Thinking," Kenyon repeated. He stepped past her and stared toward the house. "You stay here and keep thinking. I need to check things out."

The new command increased Harley's irritation. Kenyon might not *look* like a snotty kid anymore, but he could still *act* like one. "If you can go in there, I can go in," she replied. "I don't want you acting like my mother."

"I'm not going in," said Kenyon. He walked around to the passenger side of the van and pulled open the sliding door. Harley heard a series of clanks and thumps as he sorted through the tightly packed contents of the van. After a few minutes of searching, Kenyon lifted out a dark green contraption the size of a cigar box.

Harley stepped closer and squinted at the device. "What's that?"

"Infrared goggles. Former Soviet military issue." Kenyon raised the goggles to his eyes, peered toward the beach house for a moment, then scowled and lowered the device. He looked at the goggles in disgust.

"What's wrong?" asked Harley.

Kenyon shook his head. "They don't seem to be working." He fiddled with a knob on the side of the device, lifted them back to his eyes for a moment, then lowered them with a growl. "Scott was the one who knew how to work these things. I wish he was here now."

Harley agreed one hundred percent. She had been held prisoner by Unit 17 when Scott's long lost friend Chloe showed up in Stone Harbor. Harley knew how much Scott had longed to find Chloe, and she was glad they were together again, but that didn't mean she wasn't worried. Besides, she missed him.

"Can't we do without the glasses?" Harley asked. "If someone was in there, they would have to know we're out here. If they wanted to, they could have shot us both by now."

Kenyon twisted at another knob on the side of the goggles, made one last sound of disgust, then threw the device back into the van. "All right," he said. He reached up to close the door and surveyed the stacks of boxes. "You better not try to get too much stuff," he warned. "We're almost out of room."

"Don't worry," said Harley. "I don't have enough to fill a shoe box." After having had all her possessions stolen by Unit 17, Harley had barely acquired enough clothing to get her through two days. She could have had more, but that would have meant asking to borrow money from Kenyon, and she was very tired of asking for help. No matter how eager people were to give her things, to Harley it still felt like begging. If she and Kenyon did settle down in one place for some time, Harley promised herself she was going to get a job and pay her own way.

Kenyon slid the door closed on the side of the van. Then he reached inside his black leather jacket and came out with an equally black semiautomatic pistol. "All right," he said. "Let's get your things and get out of here. The sooner we're on the road, the harder it will be to locate us."

Harley wasn't sure that was true, but she was in no mood to argue. With Kenyon at her shoulder, she walked around to the front of the beach house and examined the door. It was still locked, and nothing seemed to have been touched. She pulled out her key and reached out toward the lock.

"I wouldn't do that," said a woman's voice from behind her.

Harley dropped the key onto the sand and spun around. The first thing she saw was a slender figure standing at the crest of a low dune. The second thing she saw was the red circle of Kenyon's laser sight centered on the figure's chest.

"Hold it right there," Kenyon barked. "Hands up."

A surprisingly carefree laugh came from the newcomer. "You don't want to shoot me, Mr. Moor."

Kenyon steadied the gun. "Why not?"

The figure took a step down the side of the dune, and the red spot moved from her chest to her face. In its red glow Harley could make out thin, pretty features and a long, elegant neck. "Because," the woman said. "I'm the only friend you have left."

Harley reached out and pushed Kenyon's gun to the side. "Don't shoot her," she said. She nodded toward the woman. "That's Agent Abel."

Kenyon's dark eyes stared toward the woman without blinking. "You're Abel?"

The woman laughed again. "Of course I am." She took a long step toward them and reached up to push a stray lock of hair away from her face. "Haven't Ms. Davisidaro and Ms. Janes talked about me?" she asked.

Kenyon nodded. "They have."

"And what did they say?" asked Abel as she continued

to come closer. "Charming? Beautiful? Generous to a fault?"

"They said you were a self-centered pain in the neck," replied Kenyon without lowering his gun.

Abel let out a theatrical sigh. "Really? How disappointing." Lydia Abel was a small woman, several inches shorter than Harley, and so thin she looked ready for a modeling runway. Her features were regular, smooth, and very young. If she didn't know better, Harley would have said that the woman was no more than twenty—maybe even younger than Harley herself. But the members of Abel's nameless organization had a method to rejuvenate themselves. Abel might be thirty, or fifty, or even a hundred and still look as though she just left high school.

Despite the cool night air the agent wore a thin, summer-weight silk dress covered in a design of bright flowers and twisting vines. A velvet ribbon held back her dark hair. Overall, Harley thought the woman looked as though she was ready for an elegant dinner at a fancy restaurant, not standing around on a beach.

Agent Abel walked so close to Kenyon that he was forced to move his arm to keep from jabbing her with the gun. In the moonlight Harley could see the agent's dark hair blowing in the sea breeze. The woman looked at Kenyon with an expression like a cat observing a plate of liver. "They didn't describe you, Mr. Moor. Of course, I've seen pictures, but—" She broke off, shrugged, then continued with an even wider smile. "They don't come close to doing you justice."

Harley felt irritated at the way the agent flattered Kenyon. "What are you doing here?"

Abel spoke without turning away from Kenyon. "I came here to see if you recovered from your visit with Unit 17." She glanced briefly at Harley and sniffed. "It appears you'll live. How nice."

"Yes," said Harley. "Now that you know I'm alive, you can leave." She crouched down and felt across the sand for the key. "Kenyon and I have work to do."

"In a moment, dear," Abel replied. Her blue eyes turned back to Kenyon, and she looked him up and down with obvious appreciation. "My," she said. "I knew this boy was rich, but no one told me he was so attractive."

Kenyon's dark eyes remained focused on Abel. "There's no time for this," he said. "We're in a hurry."

The agent pouted her full lips. "Handsome, but rude." She raised her hand and rested her fingertips lightly against Kenyon's arm. "Would you believe I was simply anxious to make your acquaintance, Mr. Moor? We didn't have a chance to meet earlier."

"Dee and Harley told me about you," Kenyon replied. "You're from the same organization as Ian Cain."

Abel's smile faded. "That's right. And I hold you responsible for Ian's untimely death."

"I don't care what you think," Kenyon said bluntly.

"More rudeness." Abel shook her head. "After all I've done for you, I would expect better treatment."

"And what have you done for us?" asked Harley.

Abel arched one finely curved eyebrow. "Why, Ms. Davisidaro, it was I who told Ms. Janes what had happened to you." She smiled. "I believe the phrase is, 'You owe me one.'"

"Well, I don't owe you anything," said Kenyon.

"And even if you did tell Dee what happened to Harley, I'm sure you had a selfish reason to do it. Now get out of the way." He started to move his arm away from her touch.

What happened next came so fast that Harley was never quite sure just what Agent Abel had done. One moment Kenyon was standing in front of her with a gun in his hand and a tight look on his face. Then there was a blur of movement and a cry of surprise. The second after that, Kenyon was sprawled across a dune twenty feet away and the gun was in Abel's hand.

The small, pretty woman turned the weapon over in her hands and ran a finger along the smooth metal of the barrel. "I don't tolerate rudeness," she said. A gust of wind blew up, fluttering her thin dress around the curves of her body. "Watch what you say to me, Mr. Moor."

Harley glared at her, then stepped over to Kenyon. "Are you all right?" she asked him.

Kenyon sat up and brushed sand away from his dark hair. "I'm fine," he said. His voice was tight and angry. His leather jacket creaked as he reached up and rubbed at his jaw. "This has been a long night. Let's just get your things and get out of here."

"Right." Harley turned back toward the house, but Abel stepped in her way.

"Didn't you hear me say not to go in there?" she asked.

"No," Harley replied. "I heard you say that you wouldn't go in there, but you didn't say why. I need my things."

Abel sighed. "You really are that stupid," she said.

"What a pity." She stepped out of the way and gestured at the door. "Go ahead."

Harley found her own temper rising in response to Abel's jabs, but she pressed back her anger and gave the woman a tight smile. "Thank you." She stepped past the agent and reached for the door.

"Yes, go right ahead," repeated Abel. "If you want to get yourself incinerated by a six-kilogram block of thermoplastic, be my guest."

Harley paused with the key an inch away from the lock. She turned slowly around to face the agent. "You're lying."

Abel smiled and folded her bare arms across her chest. "If you don't believe me, try it. Just don't expect to try anything else afterward."

Kenyon climbed up from the ground and stomped back to the agent. "Who would plant explosives here?" he asked.

"Unit 17," Abel responded promptly. "I watched their operatives plant the device this afternoon." She waved at the ground. "They even cleaned up their tracks. Quite a delicate operation for those brutes."

Despite being thrown across the dunes, Kenyon didn't seem ready to back down. "Unit 17 wouldn't harm Harley," he said. "They need her for their work."

"Perhaps they would find Ms. Davisidaro useful," Abel replied, "but they seem to be willing to make an exception." She held up one finger and ran it through the air as if tracing the lines of text on some invisible sheet of paper. "From Denton Bary, Acting Commander, Unit 17," she said in a dry, flat tone.

"Concerning Kathleen Davisidaro. As of this morning, we have revised our position vis-à-vis Franklin Davisidaro's daughter. Continuing losses resulting from our attempts to capture and hold Ms. Davisidaro make it imperative that we cease further such attempts. Instead we should concentrate all efforts on the immediate elimination of Ms. Davisidaro." Abel paused and wrinkled her nose. "There was more after that, but I think you'll agree we've already covered the important points."

Harley felt her heart speed up. "You saw this note? What if I don't believe you?"

Abel shrugged her thin shoulders. "You don't have to believe me. All you have to do to test my truthfulness is open that door." She took a step back. "I hope you don't mind if I move to a discreet distance first? This is a new dress, and six kilograms of C4 might leave a few scorch marks in the material."

Kenyon shook his head. "Even if there is a bomb, you could still be lying. You could have planted that explosive yourself."

The agent gave a musical laugh. "You're quite suspicious, aren't you, Mr. Moor? Good for you. But in this case I'm telling the truth."

Harley swallowed hard. "Unit 17 has really given orders to kill me?"

"Immediately, on sight, and by any means necessary," said Abel. She shook her head. "They've lost three bases to you and your friends, dear. I'm afraid they look on you with all the fondness a doctor reserves for an outbreak of Ebola."

So far, Harley had evaded Unit 17's attempts to make her part of their experiments. But Unit 17 was a military organization. Bringing in people alive wasn't their specialty. *Killing* people was much more their line. "What do we do now?" she asked. "How do I stay alive?"

Abel responded with a bright smile. "Don't ask me, dear—I have to be going myself."

"You can't go," said Kenyon.

"Oh yes, I can," Abel replied. "And by the way, this warning is another debt you owe me." She held up two fingers. "That's two, dear. I'll have to think of some way for you to repay me before you fall too deeply in debt." Agent Abel flashed a bright smile, then turned and vanished over a dune.

Kenyon watched her go and shook his head. "She's worse than Cain," he said.

Harley glanced at him. Despite Kenyon's words, there was a tone in his voice that made her think Agent Abel's charms had been more effective than Kenyon would want to admit. Harley was surprised at how bothered she felt. "What do we do now?"

Kenyon shrugged. "Do you want to try the key?"

The brass key felt cold in Harley's hand. She ran her finger over it for a moment, feeling the grooves and notches. Finally she shook her head. "No," she said. "There's nothing in there I really needed, anyway."

She turned and hurled the key as hard as she could toward the waves. It vanished without a ripple. Harley started toward the motorcycle.

"Come on," she said. "I'm done with Stone Harbor for good."

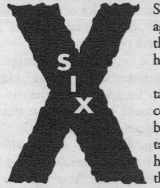

SIX

Scott tapped his pencil against the hard copy. "See, this is your problem right here."

He was seated at a folding table in the middle of the compound's communications building. Sitting across the table were Drake, who Scott had learned was in charge of the communications project, and a twentyish woman named Alice. Alice was the cooperative's expert in math and codes. They both leaned forward to see what Scott was pointing at.

"That's a one-meg encryption block," said Alice. "We use them on all our documents." She was an Asian American, with brown eyes and block-cut hair so black, it seemed almost blue. Most of the Daystar workers were constantly smiling, but Alice was not. She didn't seem very happy to have Scott poking into Umbra's security procedures.

Scott nodded. "That's right. It's a stronger key than I've seen in use anywhere else, but it's not enough."

"How can it not be enough?" asked Alice. "I studied the mathematics of cryptography in school. A one-megabyte key block should be enough to protect any message. It would take a thousand supercomputers to break that code."

"That's the theory," said Scott. "But look at the kind of messages you've been sending." He picked up a notebook computer and spun it around so the others could see the screen. "I checked the logs this morning, and it seems like you've been sending a lot of short messages. Fifty to a hundred words, does that sound right?"

Drake nodded. "Those seem typical."

"Right. Well, the way you're encoding the messages, that means almost all your primary key is wasted." He held out a sheaf of paper. "I've been looking at the relationship of text and keys. I could probably break this encryption in a week with a dozen networked PCs."

Alice did smile then, but it was a smug, self-satisfied smile. "You wouldn't have a week," she said. "We change the key block every hour. You wouldn't have enough sample to break any of the messages without a lot more number crunching."

"That's good," Scott said. "And you're probably right—it would take me a lot more than a dozen PCs. But it's not me you have to worry about, it's Legion."

Drake seemed surprised. "What does Legion have to do with computers?" he asked. "They work with animals and genetics. We've been aware that Unit 17 made certain advances in electronics, but Legion? I didn't even know they used computers."

"They have computers, all right," said Scott, "but they're not like any computers you've ever seen." He held up his hands with the palms about a foot and a half apart. "Legion is using organic brains networked together. A mass this size probably has a hundred billion interconnected neurons."

Alice's brown eyes opened wide in shock. "They've perfected neural computers?"

"Yep," Scott replied. "And I've seen them use one to break through your codes."

Alice's tan face was pulled tight in distress, and she

seemed near panic. But beside her Drake suddenly smiled brightly. "That's wonderful, Scott."

Both Scott and Alice spoke at the same time. "It is?"

Drake nodded. "A lot of people have been worried by the decision to bring you here. We understand that you have a long relationship with the Ipolex, but you also have some bad feelings for Umbra." He leaned back in his chair. "We've been worried that you might betray us to your old friends. But the way you've handled this security information shows us that you're on our side." He rocked forward and stuck out his right hand. "Congratulations, Scott, you really are one of us."

Scott felt an uneasy mix of emotions as he shook the man's hand. "Thanks."

He talked with Alice and Drake for several minutes longer, discussing possible ways to better protect Umbra's transmissions. But as soon as they left, Scott found he couldn't remember a word of what was said. All that kept playing through his head was Drake's smile and that statement: *one of us.*

Scott wasn't sure what it meant to be a member of Umbra. He had been through the ceremony twice, and each time he had experienced the raw, limitless joy of the dance and wordless songs. The people had been friendly. Chloe had been more than friendly. And now there was challenging work to do in perfecting the organization's computer and communications systems. After a lifetime of orphanages, foster homes, and boarding schools, Scott had never fit in anyplace as well as he did at Daystar.

But that didn't stop dark feelings of fear from twisting through his guts. Harley had described to him the underground chambers that Umbra had used beneath the surface of Virginia. And she had spoken of a terrible creature that lived deep in that underground lair. Those stories merged with Scott's own memories of what he had seen on the day Chloe disappeared. No matter how many smiles and handshakes he received, he wasn't sure those dark images would ever go away.

The door to the communications building opened. Scott looked up, expecting to see Drake or Alice. Instead he saw Chloe standing in the doorway.

Rather than her purple robe, she was wearing a simple blue top and faded jeans that hugged her hips tightly. Her cheeks were flushed warm pink, and her wavy hair floated around her head in a loose golden cloud. "Can I come in?" she asked.

Scott realized that he was staring at her with his mouth hanging open. "What? I mean, sure." He shoved back his chair and rose quickly to his feet. "Come on in."

Chloe glided across the small room and settled smoothly onto the chair across from Scott. "Drake told me about your discovery. It sounds like it's going to be a big help to Umbra."

"Yeah? I hope so." Scott sat down again and shook his head. "Right now all I can say is that Legion has been intercepting your transmissions and reading them. I don't know how to stop them."

"You'll figure it out," said Chloe. Her lips parted to reveal even white teeth. "I have faith in you."

For a moment Scott was paralyzed by the gentle

force of her smile. The doubts that had been plaguing him vanished like fog being steamed away by the morning sun. "Thanks," he said. "Actually, I think if we take the encryption system and make it deeper instead of just bigger, we can——" Scott's words broke off as a shiver ran through his body. A feeling of icy cold spread from his chest out into his limbs. For a moment he felt as if he was going to pass out. He swayed in his seat and pressed his palms against the table to keep from falling over.

Chloe reached across the table and grabbed Scott by the arm. "Are you all right?"

He shook his head rapidly as he tried to throw off the feeling of cold. "Yeah. Yeah, I'm fine." He flexed his stiff fingers. "I've just been feeling kind of chilly. Maybe I'm coming down with the flu."

Chloe's forehead creased in concern. "I'll see if I can get a healer to look at you this afternoon. A couple of sessions of chanting should take care of a flu."

Scott let out a laugh. "Chanting? Couldn't I just have a couple of aspirin?"

"You still don't believe, do you?" Chloe asked. The corners of her red lips turned down in a soft frown. "After everything you've seen, you would think you'd know better by now."

"It's one thing to use mental energy to affect the structure of space-time," said Scott. "It may be strange, but at least I can understand it. But using chants to kill germs?" He shook his head. "That's something I don't quite believe."

"Hmmm," said Chloe. "I'll get Emilea or Brandi to

come over here and do some chants. But if you don't believe, I'm not sure it will help."

"We'll see," said Scott. He leaned back in his chair, enjoying the chance to sit with Chloe and just talk. "What about the ceremony tonight? I can believe in what you're doing there."

Chloe's response wasn't what he hoped for. She frowned and looked away. "I'm not sure there will be a ceremony tonight."

"Why not?"

"We're not getting anywhere," Chloe said with a shrug. "Each night we come so close, but not closer. I think it's time we took a rest."

Scott felt a surge of disappointment. After only two nights of going to the ceremony, he was already looking forward terribly to a third. The thought of missing out brought a sharp sense of disappointment. "Can't we at least try?"

"There's no point," Chloe replied. "We simply don't have enough power." She was silent for a moment, then she smiled again. "Let's talk about something happier." She gestured at the electronic gear around them. "Tell me about this stuff. It looks like you've finished preparing the communications equipment."

Scott nodded. "Almost. We're still not getting a clear connection on the T3 line. I think we're going to rig some kind of amplifier."

"The lasers aren't working?"

"Oh, they're working. It's just that there's more dust in the air out here than we thought. The signal detectors at the relay station have a hard time picking up the information, so we . . . need . . . to . . . amplify. . . ." Scott's words faded, and he stared into space. Something was there—an idea that was just outside the reach of his mind.

Chloe's grip tightened on his arm. "Scott, what's wrong? Are you feeling cold again?"

"No," Scott replied. He felt a rising excitement as the plan in his mind took shape. "There's nothing wrong. In fact, I think everything may be right."

"What do you mean?"

Scott got up from the table and began to pace around the small room. He knew he was grinning like a maniac, but he was too exhilarated to care. "I'm going to need some more equipment," he said. "And some tools."

"For the laser system?" asked Chloe.

"Yes. I mean, no. I mean—" Scott stopped in his tracks and drew a deep breath. "Yeah. We need some more equipment for the laser relay, but I've got an idea for something else."

"What?"

Scott walked over and crouched down beside her so that he was looking level into her deep blue eyes. "You remember the machine I had back in Stone Harbor? The one that could detect unusual mental energy?"

Chloe nodded. "You told me about it."

"Right." Scott found himself getting so excited that he had to stop and take another breath to keep from stumbling over his words. "You said that the machine proves that the mental energy isn't magic, it's just science—like radio. You said it was like radio."

"Yes," Chloe replied. She was obviously getting confused. "Scott, what are you talking about?"

"Hang with me a second." Scott licked his lips and continued. "You know what's inside a radio?"

Chloe shrugged. "Wires and tubes?"

"And speakers, and a tuner, and *an amplifier.*" Scott leaned toward her and reached out for her hands. "Radio signals in the air are very, very faint. If the radio converted them into electricity directly, you'd never hear a thing. But the radio uses an amplifier to make those signals stronger."

He paused and waited for Chloe to catch on, but she only continued to look confused. "You already said you needed an amplifier for the laser relay. Why—"

"I'm not talking about the lasers," Scott said with a quick shake of his head. "I'm talking about the ceremony."

"I still don't see how . . ." Chloe's voice trailed away, and her eyes suddenly opened wide. "You really think you can amplify the energy of the ceremony?"

Scott nodded enthusiastically. "The detector I made took the mental energy and converted it into electricity so that it could be displayed on a screen. All we have to do is reverse the process."

Chloe jumped to her feet and threw her arms around Scott. Once again her lips pressed against his. This time the kiss lingered. Scott wrapped his own arms around Chloe and pulled her against him. For a moment he felt a joy that was as great as what he felt during the ceremony. All his doubts about what he was doing were burned away in the long seconds of the kiss. Chloe's lips seared his own. The strands of her hair seemed filled with electricity as they brushed against Scott's face.

When Chloe pulled away, her cheeks were flushed. "How long?" she asked.

It took a moment before Scott could gather enough breath to speak. "What?"

"How long will it take you to build the amplifier?"

"The amplifier . . ." Scott blinked and ran his hand across his forehead. "Um, it shouldn't be too long," he said. "I already know what I'll need."

"That's great," said Chloe. "You make a list, and I'll send someone into Rapid City right away. We'll have the equipment out here this afternoon." She gave Scott a last hug and hurried out the door.

Scott fell heavily into his chair and sat staring after her. His heart beat against his chest so hard, he thought it might break a rib. All that from a kiss, he thought. Too bad we can't catch that energy. We wouldn't even need an amplifier. Scott laughed to himself and shook his head. His feelings for Chloe were changing rapidly. The memory of the little girl from the orphanage was being worn down by the beautiful young woman who commanded Umbra. Scott would always miss the little girl, but he was beginning to think he might actually love the woman.

For just a moment his thoughts turned to Dee. Only a few days had passed since they had been together. At the time his relationship with Dee had seemed to be getting serious. Suddenly that life and his thoughts of Dee seemed dim. He still cared about her, but no moment he had experienced with Dee could match the single kiss he had received from Chloe.

Scott shook his head again. He reached across the

table to snag a pad and pencil and begin to make a list of the materials he would need to build his amplifier. But even as he was writing down grades of wire and types of switches, Scott's mind kept returning to the kiss. He tapped the end of his pencil against the pad and smiled to himself.

There might not be a ceremony tonight, he thought, but there will be Chloe. Maybe we can get out of this place for a little while and . . .

A bolt of arctic cold sliced through his thoughts. This time the freeze seemed to spread right out to the tips of his fingers and the soles of his feet. He felt stiff, frozen, caught in a web of ice. A fog spread across his vision, and for just a moment all the colors in the world seemed to drain away, leaving a world composed only of blacks and grays. Eventually the coldness passed. Warmth returned to Scott's limbs, and he found himself able to move again.

This is one weird cold, he thought. When he looked down, there were puddles of water on the table and droplets clinging to the back of his hands. It reminded him of the way drops of water condensed on a cold glass. He raised his hand, and clear water dripped off onto the table.

"Maybe a little chanting *wouldn't* be such a bad idea," he whispered to the empty room.

SEVEN

Rain slashed against her helmet's face shield as Harley guided the motorcycle around a treacherous mountain curve. The wet road sloped down steeply between a thick stand of rhododendron trees on the left and a sharp drop on the right.

All afternoon they had been working themselves down the west side of the Appalachians as they drove west and north toward Chicago. Harley led the way on the Sportster while Kenyon followed in the loaded van. And all afternoon the rain had been constant. Despite a slicker and boots Harley was soaked through. It was never pleasant to drive a motorcycle in the rain. Her blue jeans were weighed down with water that had sprayed up from the road, and sneaky raindrops were always finding gaps around her collar to send chill streams down the small of her back. At least it was warming up as she went down the long slope. Up among the mountain peaks there had been patches of sleet and damp snow mixed with the rain.

The helmet radio crackled in her ear. "I'm almost out of gas," Kenyon said from the van behind her. "What about stopping at the next town for a fill-up and dinner?"

"Sounds good," Harley replied. In fact, few things had ever sounded better. If she could talk Kenyon into abandoning the trip for the night and looking for a hotel, the world would be temporarily perfect.

It took another ten minutes to reach the bottom of the hill and five more after that to locate a small restaurant. It wasn't fancy—more a truck stop than a fine diner—but it was warm and dry. To Harley that made it ideal. She pulled her bike up to the front of the building and went inside without waiting for Kenyon. Streams of water dripped from her as she peeled off the rain slicker and draped it on the coatrack.

The small restaurant was nearly full, but as soon as Harley came through the door a pair of men in flannel shirts got up from a table and paid their bill. One of the two, a younger man with a thin mustache and a baseball cap, gave Harley a long hard look. A smile erupted on his thin face, and he turned to give her a final hungry glance as he stepped out the door. The man's expression puzzled Harley. With her hair tangled by rain and wind and her mud-splattered boots, she was definitely not at her best.

A waitress behind the counter laughed. "You get here by swimming, honey?"

"Just about," Harley replied.

The bell over the door rang as the two men left and Kenyon stepped inside. He was dressed in a smooth black cashmere sweater that matched his dark hair. He looked neat, rich, and irritatingly dry. Kenyon gave the restaurant a quick look and frowned. "Are you sure you want to eat here?" he asked. "There's bound to be a better place."

"What?" asked Harley. "You think if we go another five miles we're going to run into a little French place tucked away among the hills?" She shook her head and walked toward the nearest table. "Come on. A little real food will do you good."

Kenyon followed her to the open table and sat in one of the wooden chairs. He picked up a plastic-coated menu from the table and stared at it with obvious distaste. "I've been eating *real* food, as you so generously call it, ever since my parents died. The one thing I'm really going to enjoy about getting back home is having a chef prepare some decent meals."

Harley picked up her own menu. "What makes a decent meal?"

"The possibilities are endless." Kenyon looked up at the ceiling, and his dark eyes took on a dreamy, far-away expression. *"Brandade de morue.* Scallops *mousse-line.* Soufflé *cockaign."*

"You better not expect to get any of that stuff here," the waitress said from over his shoulder.

Kenyon turned and glanced at her. "Don't worry, I don't."

The waitress laughed. She was a broad-shouldered woman in a pink uniform. A plastic badge pinned to her dress read Marge. "Good," she said, " 'cause we don't fix anything we can't spell."

"That should limit the menu," Kenyon muttered.

Harley kicked him under the table. "Be quiet."

She ordered a burger, a plate of fries, and the largest hot coffee they had. It was far from her favorite drink, but at least it would help burn the cold and damp out of her bones. Kenyon snapped out an order, and they sat back to wait for their food.

"I don't suppose you would consider getting a

couple of rooms for the night?" Harley asked as soon as Marge brought over the hot coffee.

Kenyon shook his head. "If this is the best they can do for food in this place, I'd hate to see the hotels. Let's go on another couple of hours. That will put us close to some major cities."

"You're not the one driving the motorcycle," she said, bristling. "I'm cold and I'm tired."

"If you want me to drive the motorcycle, I will," offered Kenyon. "Or we can put it on the rack and both drive the van."

"Why didn't you say this before?"

"I did. I told you the same thing when we started out from Stone Harbor," Kenyon replied in a flat tone. "You said you wanted to drive the bike. You said you wanted to ride all the way to Chicago."

"Oh." Now that he mentioned it, Harley had to admit that she did remember saying something along those lines. "That was before I remembered how miserable a long trip on a motorcycle could be."

The waitress brought the food, and Harley was halfway through her burger when she noticed someone staring through the front window. She looked up and saw that it was the man with the thin mustache—the man who had given her the hot and heavy look. "I wonder what that guy forgot," she said around a bite of burger.

Kenyon glanced toward the window and then back at Harley. "What do you mean?"

"That man outside. He was here when we got here, but he left as soon as we came in." Harley jerked her thumb toward the window. "He must have forgotten something."

Kenyon's face went hard and cold. "Go see if this place has a back door."

Harley frowned. "What are you . . . ," she started. But before she finished her statement, she knew what Kenyon was thinking—Unit 17. "Do you have a weapon?" she asked quietly.

He shook his head. "They're all out in the van. We'll have to get outside."

"What are you going to do while I sneak out?"

Kenyon picked up his soda and took a drink. "I'm going to sit right here so it doesn't look like we're trying to escape," he said calmly. "If you find a way out, don't go alone. Wait by the door, and I'll join you in a second."

Harley was tempted to make a remark about Kenyon giving orders, but it didn't seem like the appropriate time. She pushed back her chair. As she stood she knocked her knife from the table. It clattered to the floor. Harley bent and reached for the piece of silverware.

There was a cracking sound and a high whistling buzz. A man at the next table shouted in surprise, and a coffee cup smashed to the floor.

"Down!" shouted Kenyon. "Stay down!"

Harley hesitated only a moment, then flung herself to the floor. She glanced toward the front of the restaurant and saw a line of holes in the window. The openings seemed far too neat to have been caused by any kind of bullet, but even as Harley watched, the strange whistling came again and another pair of holes appeared.

Kenyon threw himself to the tiled floor beside Harley. He shouted something, but his words were lost in the chaos. Harley could hear nothing but people screaming, glass breaking, and the thud of running feet.

Everything seemed to happen in slow motion. From her space on the floor Harley saw a forest of legs surge left and right. Almost everyone in the restaurant was up and moving. A table was overturned on her left. Dishes went flying, and glasses shattered on the tiles. A man in bib overalls stepped painfully on Harley's leg. She squirmed forward, trying to fit herself under the table. The whistling came again, and the pie rack exploded in a shower of glass.

A man with a stiff gray beard fell with blood running from a wound on his forehead.

A woman in a blue dress was flung aside like a rag doll and lay limply across one of the stools at the counter.

Harley gasped as she saw the waitress struck by the strange weapon. It didn't look like the woman had been hit by any kind of gun—it looked like she had been sliced open by an invisible sword. A bowl of chili slipped from the woman's dead fingers, and she crumbled to the ground. A crimson stain spread over her pink uniform with sickening speed. The plastic badge with the letters Marge snapped free of her dress as she fell and skittered across the floor.

"This way!" shouted Kenyon. He rose into a crouch and ran toward the kitchen.

Harley felt as if her limbs had been weighted down

by lead. She had been through danger before, and she had seen people killed. But it had never been like this. These people weren't from secret organizations—they weren't trying to hurt anyone.

Another burst of shooting was followed by a scream. She heard a sickening thump as another body fell to the floor.

I have to get out, Harley thought. I have to stop this. She climbed out from under the table, but before she could get to her feet, someone stepped on her right hand. Running feet struck her in the ribs. A boot caught her a glancing blow in the forehead.

The room swirled around Harley, and her ears rang. Another shoe kicked her arm. She curled into a ball and sheltered her head as the crowd streamed around her.

The door of the restaurant burst open. The whistling sound rose in volume, and the sound of bodies striking the floor increased to a steady patter—like stones falling down stairs. Those people who had run toward the front of the restaurant tried to reverse their direction, but it was too late. The invisible whistling beam cut them down as they ran.

Harley tried to crawl, but the wave of dead and dying passed over her like the surf crashing on the beach back in Stone Harbor. A young woman with a pink T-shirt fell across Harley's legs. A man in a business suit crashed down across her shoulders with enough force to bang Harley's head against the floor and send the room spinning.

When Harley came back to herself, the restaurant was eerily quiet. The girl in the pink shirt had the name

Jennifer stitched across her back in neat cursive letters. There were little yellow cartoon dogs around the cuffs of her sleeves and a matching yellow barrette in her hair. Harley guessed the girl was about twelve. She was dead.

Harley shivered. Everyone in the restaurant seemed to be dead. There was nothing in sight but bodies, blood, and more bodies.

Harley heard a soft crunch of glass, and a pair of legs came into view. "Do you see her over there?" asked a deep voice.

"No," a second voice replied. "You shouldn't have rushed. We were supposed to wait for backup."

"Shut up, Chris. The girl was going for some weapon under the table. I couldn't wait." The crunch of glass came closer.

Harley saw the man with the thin mustache stepping carefully through the sea of bodies. She closed her eyes and tried to still her breathing as the man drew near. Her heart was beating so loudly that it sounded like thunder in her ears. She thought the two men surely had to hear it.

"Maybe they got out," called the voice from the front of the restaurant.

"They didn't get out," replied the mustache man. "Go and get the torches. We want to get this place burning before anyone else comes along."

Harley felt the body above her shift. She dared open her eyes enough to see the man with the mustache standing almost directly above her. He was holding a thick, stubby cylinder that looked much like a soda can made from stainless steel. He raised a boot and pressed it against the man who had fallen on top of Harley. With a shove the man rolled the body off her.

A hard smile formed on the man's face. With his foot still resting on the body of the dead businessman, the killer turned toward the door. "I've found the girl!" he shouted to his partner. "I told you they didn't get away."

Harley reached out, grabbed the man's raised foot, and pushed up and back.

A brief whistle shrieked as the strange weapon fired again and plaster dust rained down from above. Then the cylinder slipped from his fingers and went bouncing into the heap of fallen people.

Harley scrambled to get to her feet, but the body of the girl in the pink T-shirt was still stretched across Harley's legs. She pulled desperately at her pinned feet.

The man with the mustache climbed upright. "You're not quite as dead as I thought," he sneered. "But we'll take care of that real quick. "Chris!" he shouted. "Get in here. We have a live one." Harley heard the sound of running feet, and a figure loomed in the doorway.

The man with the mustache turned to Harley. "Looks like this is the end for—"

There was a sharp whistle, and a clean round hole appeared in the man's forehead. With a sneer still on his face, he pitched over and died.

Harley stared toward the door in shock. Kenyon Moor waded through the sea of bodies, holding a stubby steel cylinder in his hand. "Are you hurt?" he asked.

"N . . . n . . . no," Harley stuttered. Her teeth

bounced together, and she found herself shaking so badly, it was almost like having a convulsion.

Kenyon stepped between a pair of bodies and walked closer. "We need to get moving," he said. "Someone is bound to come along in a minute, and I think they'll notice that something's wrong."

With trembling hands Harley pushed the dead girl off her legs. She climbed shakily to her feet and leaned against a table. "The . . . the other man. What happened to him?"

Kenyon scowled. "Other man?"

A flash of movement outside the shattered window caught her attention. Without stopping to breathe, Harley leaped forward and knocked Kenyon to the ground.

They landed among the bodies just as the whirring noise sounded from the front of the restaurant. Harley pushed herself away from the bloody body of a dead man in time to see a line of white floor tiles explode less than a foot away from her face.

"Stay down!" Kenyon barked. He rolled off a body and rose to one knee with his pistol in his hand, but before he could fire, the strange gun whirred again. A thin line of blood arced away from Kenyon's arm and the black pistol slipped from his hand.

Harley's heart raced as the gun clattered to the floor. She could see Kenyon's mouth working as he called out some curse, but she heard nothing. All sound had faded away.

From the corner of her eye she saw the second killer step back into the restaurant. His lean face was twisted by a savage grin, and the thick, stubby gun was clamped in his hand. He raised the weapon and sprayed a burst of fire toward Harley and Kenyon.

A red mist closed over Harley's vision. With the shots falling around her, she reached down and picked up Kenyon's gun. The pistol was large in her hand. Heavy. Deadly.

Something stung at the side of her leg. A fragment of broken plate cut into her cheek. Harley didn't pause. She rose up with the gun in her hand, turned, and walked straight toward the man. Her finger tightened around the trigger of the semiautomatic pistol.

The gun kicked in her hand, but there was still no sound.

The man who had given her the hungry look was wearing a very different look now. His eyes went wide, and his mouth opened to reveal very even white teeth.

Harley fired again. The bullet caught the man in the chest and drove him back through the door of the restaurant. His white teeth were stained with blood.

Harley followed.

The man was on the porch. He still held the strange gun in his right hand, but he wasn't trying to use it. His flannel shirt was dark and plastered to his body.

Harley shot him again, and the man tumbled off the porch into the rain-soaked parking lot. The gun bucked and kicked as Harley squeezed the trigger over and over and over.

A hand landed on Harley's arm.

She whirled, her face and muscles tight with rage.

Sound and sensation returned in a rush. "He's dead," said Kenyon. "Harley. He's dead."

Harley realized that she was standing in the pouring rain with a dead man at her feet. There was pain in her leg and in her face, but she couldn't remember why. "What . . . why . . ." She searched for words that wouldn't come.

Kenyon pried the empty pistol free from Harley's numb fingers. "Come on," he said. "I think we better get out of here."

Harley nodded mutely. She breathed in hard gasps. Halfway across the wet parking lot those gasps turned into sobs. She leaned against the bike and closed her eyes before the sobs could turn into screams.

Scott threw the soldering iron onto the table. "This won't do," he said. "If I try to put components into the system with that thing, I'll end up frying the whole board."

"This is the best thing we could find," said Drake.

"I'm sorry." Scott shrugged. "It's just not going to work."

After a day of discussing plans they were back in the communications hut. All other parts of the project had been put on hold while Scott worked on his amplifier. A stack of supplies had been delivered to help with the project, but more than a few of the parts were unsuitable.

Drake frowned, and the curving scar on his forehead turned a deep red. "All right," he said. "We'll send someone to look for a better tool."

"I could go," offered Scott. "It would probably be best if I picked it out myself."

The idea seemed to distress Drake. He got up from the table and shook his head. "I don't think that's a good idea. The Ipolex tells me that you've been feeling ill."

"It's nothing serious," said Scott. "Just a little cold." But even as he spoke, another bout of chills came over him.

He had felt the waves of cold frequently through the night. In between bouts of cold Scott had suffered through short spells of dark, disconnected dreams full

93

of shifting chaotic images. Chloe had visited those dreams, but he'd dreamed about others, too—silent midnight figures that left Scott shivering as much from fear as from cold. He would wake up from one of the dreams sweating, then find himself in the grip of a fresh round of icy shivering. By the time the sun rose, Scott felt far weaker and more tired than when he had gone to bed.

Scott recovered from the latest shot of arctic cold and found that Drake had gone. He slumped across the table and closed his eyes. He felt so horribly tired. He was sure that the amplifier would work, but if he didn't get some medicine soon, he wasn't sure he would be in any shape to help build the device.

The door to the building swung open, and Chloe stepped inside. At her first sight of Scott, she bit her lip. "Drake said you were feeling worse."

Scott started to protest, but instead he nodded. "Yeah, I feel pretty bad."

Chloe held open the door for another woman. "This is Emilea. She's a healer."

Scott waved. "Hi. I guess I'm the healee." He still didn't believe that anyone could cure a cold by chanting at it, but as bad as he felt, he was willing to let the woman try.

The healer was middle-aged, with a thick mass of dark brown curls and soft gray eyes. Instead of walking straight to Scott, she circled him with her hands outstretched. Every few steps she gave a little shuffle or hop. She held out her hands and shook her fingers as if she were shaking off water.

Despite how poorly he felt, Scott had to hold back laughter at the healer's antics. "What are you doing?"

"I'm measuring the energy lines radiating from your aura," the healer replied seriously.

"Right," said Scott. He leaned forward and looked through the door. "Is someone out there with a jar of leeches?"

Chloe rolled her blue eyes. "Joke all you want. Emilea is a powerful healer. If you give her a chance, she'll take care of your problem."

Scott nodded and leaned back. "After the night I had, I'm ready to try the leeches."

The healer made another orbit of Scott and the table, then stopped beside Chloe. "It is as you suspected," she pronounced in a low voice. "The immersion has exceeded his limits."

"What does that mean?" Scott asked.

"Shhh," said Chloe. She frowned at the healer. "Can you reverse the situation?"

"Uncertain," the woman replied. "But we should be able to slow the process through reversal of axis."

"Then let's do it," said Chloe. She walked around behind Scott and placed her hands on his shoulders while the healer stood in front of him with her arms raised above her head.

"Wait a minute!" Scott broke in. "Can someone tell me what all that meant—"

Before Scott could finish his sentence, a current of incredible electricity flowed out of Chloe's hands and into his neck and shoulders. Pain and fear were carried away as Scott found himself riding a geyser of energy.

Blue fire seared along his nerves, but it was a warming, comforting fire. He lost all sight and sense of the room around him as he sank into a vortex of power. The swirling lines of energy carried him down to an electric sea where geometric shapes unfolded and reformed a thousand times a second. Points stretched into lines, lines expanded into squares, squares grew into cubes, and cubes extended into multidimensional shapes for which Scott had no name.

Scott had heard Harley talk about the visions sent by her paranormal abilities—the artificial world that Noah had created within the sphere, the tangled nexus where dreams swirled together, flashing fragments of the past and future—but Scott had never seen anything like that. Like the powers of the healer, he had never been sure he even believed in these paranormal visions. In the lake of fire Scott became a believer.

At first there was nothing but the geometric shapes. They repeated and mixed and spun through every possible combination. There were patches of color from black to red to searing white. It seemed to Scott that some meaning was hidden in the shapes and colors, but he couldn't quite make it out. It was like a coded computer message.

Then it was as if the camera in Scott's mind began to move farther and farther back. The clusters of shapes moved together until whole groups of shapes were reduced to a pinpoint. All the nonsense that Scott had fought to understand became crystal clear. It was a face.

Dee Janes looked at him from the depths of his mind.

Scott tried to talk. He wanted to ask Dee what she

was doing in his mind. But he had left his body outside. He could make no sound.

The image zoomed back again. Dee's face shrank to the size of a postage stamp, then a pinprick, then nothing. And then rational thought was gone along with sight, sound, and touch.

Sometime later—maybe minutes, maybe hours, maybe days—Scott found himself drifting up out of the depths. The infinite layers of geometric shapes splashed off him like cool water. Gradually the real world took shape around him, and he realized that he was still sitting in a chair in the communications room. Chloe and the healer were talking together on the other side of the table. He rubbed his eyes and tried to shake the cobwebs out of his head. "How long was I out?" he asked.

Chloe grinned. "About ten seconds."

"Is that all? It sure felt longer." An image floated through his mind. It was an image of a face, but the more Scott concentrated on trying to make out the features, the harder it became.

"How do you feel?" Chloe asked. "Any more of the cold spells?"

The image in Scott's mind lost shape and melted away like a sand castle at high tide. Scott blinked and returned Chloe's smile. "I'm fine." He flexed his fingers. The stiffness that had plagued him for the last day seemed to be gone. "What did you do?"

"We reversed your internal astral field axis to bring it in line with the local vortex," replied the healer.

"I guess I'm going to have to believe in that stuff

after all," said Scott. "But it still sounds crazy." He stood up and rubbed his hands together. He not only felt better, he felt energized. He felt ready to get to work and ready to get something accomplished. "I think I'll start on the energy collection part of the amplifier."

"I thought you needed some new tools," said Chloe.

Scott nodded. "I do, but I'll see what I can do with the material we already have."

Chloe smiled at the news. She brushed her fingers lightly against Scott's face and then stood. "Come on, Emilea. Let's leave the genius at his work." The healer rose, made a short bow, and hurried out the door. Chloe moved to follow but stopped in the doorway. "If you start feeling bad again, let me know right away."

"It's a deal," said Scott. He reached up and touched the place where Chloe had put her hands on his shoulders. He almost expected the skin to be bruised or burned, but it felt normal. "The treatment felt so good, I think I might call you even if I *don't* start feeling bad."

Chloe's grin took on a mischievous edge that Scott remembered from childhood. "Careful," she warned. "That's how people get addicted. Besides, I can think of other things that would feel good." She stepped out and let the door slam.

Scott stared at the wooden door for long seconds after she left. He swallowed hard. The confusion he had felt about Chloe was fading away, but in its place a desire was rising. Scott wished he could get up and follow Chloe back to her room.

Work, he thought. Work now. Chloe later. He

turned his attention to the collection of electronic parts on the table, but he found it hard to push away thoughts of blue eyes, and golden hair, and red lips.

For the next hour Scott tore into the design for his amplifier. It wasn't as easy as it seemed when he'd first thought of the idea. Detecting the paranormal energy was one thing, producing it was a much more difficult problem. He realized that he was facing some of the same problems that one of the other secret groups had already tackled. Unit 17 had tried to produce paranormal energy by using a machine to amplify the output of a single mind. To make their system work, Unit 17 had been forced to create a structure that filled buildings and held electronics so advanced that they were like something from another world. Only the genius of Harley's father had allowed them to create the device at all.

It seemed ridiculous to even think that Scott could match Unit 17's massive creations with a few home-made circuit boards and parts salvaged from radios and computers. In fact, the more calculations he did, the more Scott realized that the output of his device would be tiny. The conversion of electricity into paranormal power would be terribly inefficient. Even if everything worked perfectly, he might be able to increase the output of the circle by only one or two percent. But one percent might be enough. Unit 17 was producing its energy from one person. Umbra was using many minds joined together in the energy of the ceremony. Umbra was already so close to producing the white sphere without any help that Scott's tiny addition might be all they needed to tip them over the edge.

Scott reached out across the table and picked up a fat orange capacitor. As he stared at the chunk of wire and ceramic, the final outlines of the machine he would build began to become clear in his mind. Most of what he needed could be made from the parts on the table, but there was one thing missing. If he was going to gather in the paranormal energy and amplify it, he would need a collector—an antenna for his magic radio.

Scott thought for a moment and remembered the satellite uplink dish. It had a wire mesh antenna almost ten feet across. The dish might be exactly what he needed.

Leaving all the small electronics parts scattered across the table, Scott got up and went outside. After hours of sitting in the windowless communications shed, he found himself squinting against the fierce afternoon sun. He had spent so much time in the building for the last few days that coming out almost seemed like coming out of a cave.

Still energized by his session with the healer, Scott turned and marched toward the ridge where the satellite dish was perched. The hillside was steep, and the soft clay stone crumbled easily, but Drake and the others on the communications project had worn a smooth path from the shed to the ridge top that Scott followed easily.

The satellite uplink sat on the capstone of the ridge like an overgrown flower of metal. Scott ran his hand along the steel mesh of the sides and looked at the arm that jutted out into the focal point to broadcast Umbra's transmissions to the sky. The central electronics package would have to be replaced, of course, but the rest of the device seemed salvageable. The focus of the dish would need to be adjusted. Scott leaned in for a better look at how the petals of the metal flower were connected.

Brother.

The word seared through Scott's mind like a needle of ice. He staggered back and grabbed the metal lip of the dish to keep from falling. "What?"

Brother. Join us.

As if drawn by some huge magnet, Scott staggered to the other side of the ridge and looked down. A line of figures stood at the base of a ragged cliff face. They wore the smooth purple robes of Umbra, and they were all looking up, their faces tilted toward Scott. Only they had no faces. Inside the hood of each robe was only a space of infinite, impenetrable darkness.

"What . . . what are you?" whispered Scott.

Despite the distance the faceless creatures seemed to hear his soft words. *We are your brothers,* they replied. Their voices echoed through Scott's head like an unholy chorus. Moving as smoothly as a line of dancers, the robed figures took a step toward the base of the cliff and raised their arms. The sleeves of their robes seemed as empty as their hoods.

Join us, they sang. *Come share in our brotherhood.*

A buzzing echoed in Scott's mind like a hive of bees gone wild. "Yes," he breathed. "Yes, I'm coming." He spread his arms and stepped into the air.

In Harley's dreams she lived through the massacre in the restaurant again and again.

A dozen times she saw the girl in the pink T-shirt with the cartoon dogs fall down like a puppet with the strings cut. She saw the waitress with her big plastic name tag and the man in the business suit who had died and fallen on Harley. He had saved her life. The man in the business suit had saved Harley's life, and she didn't know his name. She had never even seen his face. There was only the cheap brown suit.

And blood. On everything there was blood. She moaned and reached out, trying to push away the awful visions.

She woke in the front seat of the van.

"Are you okay?" asked Kenyon. The tone of his voice was dry, and he kept his eyes fixed on the highway ahead.

Harley nodded without speaking and ran her fingers through the tangled mass of her dark hair. It was still raining, and the windshield wipers on the van squeaked back and forth across the glass. The Sportster was in its cradle at the back of the van, and all the supplies salvaged from Stone Harbor were crammed into the space behind them. Outside, the landscape had lost its hills. There were only flat fields separated by lines of standing timber and a few farmhouses surrounded by clusters of barns and outbuildings.

"Where are we?" Harley asked.

"Southern Indiana," Kenyon replied. "We'll be crossing over into Illinois any minute."

Harley nodded. She couldn't shake the awful images of her dream. "How many people?" she asked softly.

"What?"

"At the restaurant," Harley said. "How many people do you think they killed?"

Kenyon was silent for a second. "Somewhere between twenty and twenty-five," he said. "The place was full, but it was small."

Twenty-five people. Twenty-five people who had been killed just because Unit 17 was trying to get rid of Harley. She shifted in her seat and looked at Kenyon. "Maybe I should just turn myself in."

"Don't be ridiculous," said Kenyon. "They'd only kill you, and that wouldn't help anything."

"And if I don't turn myself in, how many more people are going to die?" she asked.

Kenyon shook his head. "It's not your fault that they died. You didn't kill them."

Harley ran her hands across her face and was surprised to find no tears on her cheeks. "I feel like I did," she said.

"Don't," Kenyon said sharply. "If you hadn't taken out that last guy, there would have been two more dead. You did well."

His cold tone jarred Harley. "Don't you feel anything?" she demanded. "Doesn't it bother you?"

Kenyon glanced away from the road and looked her straight in the eye. "It bothers me," he said. "Unit

103

17 killed all those people, and they killed my parents, and they took your father and your friend Noah, and who knows what else they've done. But I'm not going to let them win." He bared his teeth, but it wasn't a smile. It was more like a snarl. "Revenge," he said in a rough voice. "Revenge is the only answer." He turned his attention back to the road and steered the van around a slow-moving rental truck.

Harley leaned away from him and rested her cheek against the cool glass of the side window. Through the ghost of her own reflection, she watched the wet, empty fields slide past. Part of her wished she could be like Kenyon. From the very beginning he had turned every wound into anger. Whenever Unit 17 or one of the other secret groups caused him pain, Kenyon resolved to give them even more pain in return.

But it wasn't pain that Harley wanted. She had no desire for revenge. All she wanted was Noah back, and her father back, and her life back to normal. She wanted Marge the waitress, and the girl in the pink T-shirt, and the man in the cheap brown suit to get up and finish their meals and go on with their lives.

Harley closed her eyes. Her turbulent dreams had given her no rest, and she still felt exhausted. Once they reached Kenyon's home, she thought she might sleep for a month. Maybe that would be long enough for the dreams to end—but she doubted it.

As sleep closed in around her a point of light appeared in the darkness. It swelled and took on a golden tone that spread around Harley and brought her down to a soft landing. Harley found herself standing in a field of yellow timothy beneath a faded denim sky. There were round-shouldered heaps of hay along the edge of the field, and a hundred yards away rows of corn had been bundled into sheathes. In the distance a forest of oak, and elm, and hickory was alive with the bright colors of fall.

Harley breathed the sweet, dry air and felt a sense of calm drop like a blanket across her troubled thoughts. Ever since Noah had carried Harley's dying father into the white sphere, he had been bringing Harley to this place of dreams. Noah had said that the whole place was only a creation of his mind, but Harley had seen seasons come and go across the dream landscape. She couldn't imagine how anything so real could be the result of one person's illusions. And on her last trip to the place Harley had seen her own mother walking through the trees. If Noah's world was a dream, it was a dream that others shared.

"Noah!" she called across the fields. "Are you here?"

"Yes," came a voice from close behind her. "Right here."

Harley turned and saw Noah Templer standing amid the high grass. On her last visit he had been without any shirt, but now he wore a rough vest of undyed cotton. A broad-brimmed hat was perched on his thick blond hair, held in place by a leather cord that tied beneath his chin.

"What's with the new clothes?" she asked.

Noah put one finger under the brim of his hat, tilted it back, and glanced up at the sky. "It might be fall in this place, but the sun is still pretty fierce. I kept getting burned."

"I thought this was all your imagination."

Noah shrugged. "Even imaginary sunburn stings."

Harley started to laugh, but the laughter died in her throat. "Noah. Back in . . . outside of here. Something terrible happened."

"I know." He stepped toward her with his arms held open.

Harley walked into his arms and let Noah fold her against his chest. It had been a long time since Harley had felt the need to be cradled—not hugged, just held and protected. But she needed it now. "How can you know what happened?" she whispered.

She felt Noah's shoulders shrug against her arms. "Most of the time I can't see beyond the sphere, but sometimes—especially when something important happens—I get a peek outside."

"What are we going to do?" Harley asked. "How did things ever get this way?"

Noah leaned down and pressed his face into the dark fall of Harley's hair. "Things are about to change," he said.

"Change how?"

"I can't tell that yet," Noah replied. "But things are different in here."

Harley leaned back so she could look into his face. "Different how?"

Noah stood still for a moment. Then he took his arms from around Harley, reached down into the grass, and pulled out a small white flower. It was a tiny daisy, with a bright yellow center and a ring of snowy petals. He held it out to Harley. "Here, take a look."

The flower seemed to tremble as Harley t̶ from his hand. She raised it up for a better look, before she could bring the bloom near her face, the whole flower wavered, became translucent, and burned away like fog under strong sunshine.

Harley opened her empty hand and looked at Noah. "Why did you do that?"

"I didn't," he said. "This place is falling apart." He spread his arms to take in the world around them. "It's getting harder and harder for me to hold it together. Sometimes I can't keep it going at all."

"Why?" asked Harley. "I thought you were getting better at creating this world."

"I was," said Noah. "But that was before the neighborhood got so crowded." Behind him the distant trees of the forest suddenly twisted and swayed. Leaves turned black, and branches clawed the ground like fingers. Then the whole forest vanished, leaving behind a patch of earth as blank and gray as a concrete parking lot.

Harley tried to make some sense out of Noah's words and the strange sights. "What do you mean, crowded?" she asked. "There's no one here but you."

Noah shook his head. "It only seems that way." He frowned in thought for a moment, then pointed over Harley's shoulder. "Look over there."

She turned and was amazed to see a globe of the earth spinning silently above the ground a dozen feet away. She walked closer. It was more than a globe. It was a perfect image of the blue earth, just as she had seen it in shots from space. "Why show me this?"

"Keep looking," said Noah.

A white ball appeared next to the earth. For a moment Harley thought it was the moon, but this ball was as large as the earth, and it stood so close that the surface of the ball and the earth almost touched. "That's the white sphere," Noah explained. "Or at least that's what's inside it."

"I don't—" started Harley.

"I know," Noah interjected. "Hang on. I think it'll start to make sense in a minute."

The white ball began to roll around the earth. It moved faster and faster, tracing up and down, looping around the poles, then swinging down to the equator. Eventually the sphere was moving so fast that it was nothing but a white blur, holding the earth inside its pale cloud. "That's the best I can do," said Noah. "The inside of the white sphere is a separate world—maybe a whole separate universe—but it touched ours. You go in one place, you can come out in another. You see?"

Harley nodded. "I can see that much."

"Good. Now imagine there are other spheres around the first one." The white sphere slowed its mad pace around the earth and was joined by another ball of brilliant green, then a sphere of red, then one of blue. These new spheres orbited around the white sphere in the same way the white sphere orbited around the earth. As the image returned to its previous mad speed, the whole contraption became a furious blending of color and movement with the blue earth trapped in the center.

"What's in those other spheres?" Harley asked.

"I don't know," said Noah. "I've never been there." The scale of the model changed. The earth shrank to the size of a tennis ball, then to a blue marble, then to a point. But as it shrank, the cloud of whizzing, rolling spheres only grew. "There are a lot of other spheres, Harley. Maybe a thousand. Maybe an infinite number. But in a way they all touch one another everywhere at the same time. Does that make any sense?"

Harley felt dizzy as she looked at the insane model. "No," she said. "Not at all."

Noah shrugged. "It doesn't make much sense to me, either. But the important part is that only the white sphere touches the universe where the earth lives. You can't get there without going through here."

"I can't say I understand that, either," said Harley. She turned away from the tumbling spheres and looked at Noah. "Where did you learn all this?"

A sad expression crossed his face, and he turned his blue eyes away. "From your father."

"My father?" Harley felt a rush of excitement. "My father is here?"

Noah shook his head. "He was here, but he's been gone for some time."

"Where did he go?" Harley asked breathlessly. "Is he still alive?"

"I'm not sure." Noah waved his hand, and the motion of the complex model stopped. Frozen in place, it looked like a million soap bubbles all resting together in a great mass of color and light. "I think he was forced into another sphere."

"Who forced him?" asked Harley.

Overhead the sky went from blue to a sickly yellow, then to a featureless flat gray. Noah looked at it, and his lips tightened in concern. "We're going to have to hurry," he said. "I can't hold this place much longer."

Harley stepped toward him. "My father," she cried. "What happened to my father?"

Noah nodded. "When we first came into the sphere," he said quickly, "there were a lot of people in this place. There were your father and some of Unit 17's test subjects." He paused, and his face took on a sour expression. "And even Commander Braddock."

"What happened to them?" asked Harley.

"I can't be sure," Noah replied. A stiff breeze blew up. It sent waves through the grass and knocked Noah's hat back on his head. A roar rose in the distance like an approaching hurricane. "It was hard for us to communicate," Noah shouted above the rising gale. "Then the others started coming."

"What others?" Harley shouted back.

"The ones from outside." The field behind Noah rippled and was replaced by another patch of featureless gray. "They came here from another sphere and started pushing the other people out. Your father and all the rest are gone. I'm the only one who managed to hang on."

Harley stumbled. She looked down at her feet and found the yellow timothy gone. The bundles of corn and even the sweet scent of fall had gone. In their place was only the gray and the endless rushing, crackling, roaring sound.

"What are they?" she screamed, hoping to be heard above the noise.

Noah himself seemed to be fading away. She could barely make out his face as he shook his head. "They're big," he replied. "Really big." He reached out toward her, and Harley saw that his hands were as pale and translucent as the fading flower.

"Noah!" she called. "What's happening?"

His mouth moved, but his words were almost lost in the howling of the void. ". . . lands. Badlands."

Harley frowned. "What?"

"Are you awake?"

Harley opened her eyes to find herself still in the front seat of the van. The rain outside the windows had stopped, but from what Harley could see, the landscape remained much the same. "Yeah," she replied to Kenyon's question. "I guess so." She pushed herself away from the window. Sleeping in the front seat of the van had left her with a crick in her neck and a taste in her mouth like something had died. "Where are we now?"

"Halfway up Illinois," said Kenyon. "We're about four hours from Chicago. I'm going to pull over and get some gas. Do you want something to eat?"

Harley winced at the question. "Maybe it would be better if we hit a drive through."

"Right," Kenyon agreed. He pulled off at the next exit and slid up to the pumps of a large gas station.

Harley sat in the van for a few minutes as Kenyon filled the tank. She tried to remember her dream of Noah, but like all her trips to the dream world, the images were faint and fuzzy when she woke. She could vaguely remember Noah explaining to her the

111

structure of the spheres, but the details of the conversation were lost.

A bank of pay phones at the corner of the lot caught her eyes. Harley dug into the back pocket of her jeans and pulled out a wrinkled business card. She swung open the door and stepped down out of the van. "Everything going okay?" she called to Kenyon.

He nodded in reply. "So far. There are a couple of fast-food places down the block. We can grab something there and be back on the road in a few minutes. By midnight we can be at my home."

Harley still wasn't sure how she felt about the idea of staying at Kenyon's house. But at the moment the thought of sleeping in a warm bed overcame any other concern. She walked closer to Kenyon and spoke in a lower voice. "I'm going to go make a call to Stone Harbor."

"Why?" asked Kenyon.

"I want to check on Zombie Express," Harley replied. "Maybe Legion has coughed up some information on Scott and Chloe."

Kenyon scowled. "I wouldn't count on it," he said. "I wouldn't count on any of the organizations keeping their word."

"It won't hurt to check." Harley turned and started toward the phones.

"Don't stay on too long!" Kenyon called after her. "Three minutes, tops."

Harley nodded. She doubted that Unit 17 was checking every call that came into the Stone Harbor Police Department, but after what had happened on the trip, she was afraid that Kenyon might be right. Unit 17 seemed to be willing to go to any lengths to find and kill Harley.

She dialed the phone number on the card and waited while the phone clicked and rang. It was picked up almost right away.

"Stone Harbor Police Department. Is this an emergency?"

"No, it's . . ." Harley paused. She wasn't sure what to say. "It's Kathleen Vincent," she said at last, giving the false name that was on all the identification she carried.

"Hang on," said the voice on the line. "The chief's been waiting for your call."

A moment later Harley heard Mr. Janes's voice. "Harley? Is that you?"

"It's me," Harley said quickly. "I was just wondering if—"

But Mr. Janes spoke again before Harley could ask about the message. "Where is she?"

"Where is who?" Harley asked in surprise.

"My daughter," replied the police chief. Even from a thousand miles away Harley could hear the mixture of fear and anger in Chief Janes's voice. "Dee is gone."

**TEN**

Voices rose up to Scott from a sea of darkness.

"How long was he with them?" asked a woman's voice.

"Not long," a man's voice replied. "Five minutes. Maybe a little more."

Scott felt nothing. The voices seemed like the lines of actors on some distant stage. He felt no emotion at their words. He wasn't even concerned about who they were. The darkness was all he needed.

"Can you reverse it?"

"I'm not sure." It was a new voice. Another woman. "He's gone a long way along the path."

"We need to have him back." The first woman. Even from the darkness Scott could hear the anger in her voice. "He's no good to us like this."

"He will serve," said the man's voice. "Just as the others do."

"We need his skills, not more mindless muscle. Tell Void that he and the rest of them must stay away until after tomorrow's ceremony."

"Void doesn't listen to me," replied the man.

"Then talk to Zero. He's the youngest. He still understands what it means to breathe."

The sound of the door opening and closing again. Scott began to feel bored. He swam deeper into the darkness, where the voices were only a faint nuisance in the distance. It seemed to him that there was a cold, secret heart at the very bottom of the black lake in which his mind moved. That frozen core promised to take away the voices and the last traces of the confusing world.

Fingers of ice reached up from the black heart of nothingness to grab him.

Then suddenly he was surging upward. Hands of burning fire held him by the throat and dragged him away from the black core. Like a fish being pulled from a lake, he was torn away from the darkness and thrown back into the world of light and sensations.

Scott opened his eyes. At first everything around him was fuzzy, but as his eyes regained their focus, he found himself back in the communications building, seated across the cluttered table from Chloe and the healer, Emilea.

Chloe smiled at him. "Feeling better?" she asked.

"I . . . I don't know." Scott blinked and tried to shake the foggy feeling out of his head. "What happened?"

"Emilea performed a healing to send away the illness you've been having."

Scott nodded. "I remember that. What happened after?"

The two women exchanged a puzzled look. "What do you mean?" asked Chloe. "We just finished the healing."

Scott shook his head. "No. You did the healing, and we talked, and then I worked on the amplifier." His memories became sketchy, and he paused for a moment to collect his thoughts. "Then I went outside to see the . . . satellite dish. That's right, the dish. I went up the hill, and . . . and . . ." Scott stopped and shook his head again. "I don't remember anything after that."

Chloe reached across the table and patted the back of his hand. "Dreams, Scott. Those were only dreams."

"Dreams?"

The healer spoke up. "The healing ceremony commonly produces dreams. It's nothing to worry about."

Scott rubbed at his eyes. "But it seemed so real."

"I'm sure it did," said Chloe. "But the important question is, do you feel better? Are the cold feelings gone?"

Scott nodded uncertainly. He flexed his hands and tested the muscles of his shoulders. "Yeah, I think so."

"Good." She pushed back her chair and stood. The healer moved fast to stand beside Chloe. "We'll get out of here and leave you to your work. If you start to feel ill again, be sure to call. All right?"

"I guess so," Scott replied.

With a last smile Chloe led the healer out of the building and closed the door.

For minutes after they left, Scott sat in his chair and stared across the room. He tried to put together the pieces of his strange dream. He had been on top of a hill, and there had been people—people made of nothing but night. He remembered flying, and people talking to him, and voices in his mind. Finally he shook his head and laughed. Like all dreams, this one didn't hold together once he tried to examine it.

He thought for a moment about going up to inspect the satellite dish. It would be needed to complete the device. But going up the hill seemed like a bad idea. Instead Scott picked up a pad of paper and a mechanical pencil from the table and started plotting exactly how he would finish his amplifier.

A few minutes later the door opened and the man called Drake stepped in. He had two shopping bags full of supplies in his arms and a big smile on his square-jawed face. "I've got goodies," he said. "I think you're going to be pleased this time."

Scott helped unpack the new supplies and examined the materials. There were coils of gleaming wire, boxes of capacitors, resistors, and lead solder—and a whole new set of tools. "This looks like good stuff," said Scott. "We should be able to make exactly what we need."

"That's great." Drake sat down beside Scott and looked at the sketches and equations on Scott's pad. "No one here has ever tried to do anything like this. You think you can tell me some of the theory behind what you're doing?"

Scott shrugged. He was used to working alone, and he felt a little uncomfortable working with others, but he couldn't see any reason to say no. "Sure," he said. "I'll tell you what I can."

"That's great," Drake repeated. "Just great."

For hours after that, Scott worked and tinkered on his device. To his own surprise, he found he liked talking about the work. On Drake's part, he took pages of notes and covered more pages with sketches of Scott's growing amplifier. He seemed very interested in the work, and he was more than eager to help by holding a circuit board or handing Scott a tool. Scott had been worried that explaining his work to

Drake would slow him down, but instead he found the work going very well.

They had finished off one breadboard and started a second when Alice came in. "The Ipolex wants to know if you're going to have an evening meal," she said.

Scott shrugged. "I guess so, when it's time."

Alice pointed toward the open door. "It's long past evening meal. Most of the members have already gone to their quarters for the night."

Scott was surprised to see that the sky outside was completely dark. He looked over at Drake. "I'm sorry to keep you out here so late."

"No problem." Drake closed his notebook and rubbed his forehead above the thin scar. "It looks like we've outlined the whole device."

"Everything but the collector," said Scott. "We'll need something to act as an antenna. Something like the . . . the . . ." An image flashed across his mind. He saw the dish from the satellite uplink, but he also saw a line of faceless men in robes.

A hand closed on Scott's arm. "Hey, you all right?"

Scott nodded quickly. "Fine. I was just saying we needed something like the satellite dish to act as a collector."

"We can take care of that," said Drake. "I'll disconnect the dish and have it down here first thing in the morning."

"Good." Suddenly the energy that had carried Scott through the afternoon seemed to drain away. He swayed in his seat. "I think I'm going to crash."

Both Drake and Alice looked at him with concern. "You need any help?" asked Alice.

Scott stood and shook his head. "No. I'm fine. All I need is a little sleep."

He stumbled past both of them and out into the night. The buildings of the Daystar Cooperative were dark, and there was no one left in the field. Scott wondered just how late it really was. He made his way to his single room, sat down on the edge of the bed, and peeled off his shirt. Scott shivered slightly in the cool breeze, but the fresh air felt good. It was certainly warmer than the flashes of arctic cold that had come over him the night before.

Images from the strange dream he had experienced during the healing kept stirring in his mind. Even more than the images, it was the feelings. The emotions from the dream seemed like a strange echo of the feelings from the ceremony. Both had been nearly perfect, and both had made him feel completely free from all the confusion and pain in his life. But the ceremony had been pure joy, and the dream had been pure darkness. Not hate or anger, just a yawning, bottomless cavern that held no emotion.

Scott felt disappointed that Chloe hadn't waited up for him. Even if what had happened during the healing was only a dream, it would have been good to talk to Chloe about these strange emotions. Besides, he wanted to spend more time with her. After the kiss she had given him earlier, Scott wanted to get her away from the compound and be alone with her. It was going to be tough to build a relationship unless they could get away from this strange place.

For a moment Scott thought of going over to

Chloe's room and seeing if she was still awake. As the leader of Umbra, she had a far larger apartment than anyone else, and her rooms were right across the hall.

Still trying to decide what to do, Scott lay back on the bed and closed his eyes. A few minutes passed before he realized that even though his eyelids were completely closed, he could still see the room around him. Quickly Scott opened his eyes, then closed them again. He could see the plain square table and the single wooden chair. He could even see the slender spire of the radio tower rising outside the window.

Scott got up from the bed and turned slowly around. Not only could he see the room with his eyes shut, he could actually see it better than he could with his eyes wide open. There was no color, but every detail of the dark room stood out as clear as day. There seemed to be an impossible number of shades of gray, and the textures of everything seemed subtly different—as if the world were made from slivers of bone and fragments of iron.

A fresh wave of cold passed through Scott. This time the icy feeling shot through him like an electric current. He could feel the glacial chill working its way into his bones. His heart jumped, twitched madly, then grew quiet. For the space of a second it seemed to lie in his chest like a lump of cold stone, then it jerked painfully and resumed a steady beat.

Scott pulled in a ragged breath. "What's happening to me?" he asked the empty room. His breath came out in a chill fog.

He spun, hurried to the door, and flung it open. In one step he crossed the hallway and pounded his fist against the plain wooden panel that blocked the entrance to the Ipolex's chambers. "Chloe!" he shouted. "Chloe! Something's wrong with me. I need help."

The wooden panel slid to the side, and Scott almost cried in relief when he saw Chloe looking out at him. She was dressed in her purple robe, and her hood was raised. It cast shadows over her face and made her blue eyes seem darker. "Do you feel cold again?"

Scott nodded. "Yes," he said. "It's worse. I feel like I'm turning into ice."

Chloe gave a soft sigh. "I had hoped it would be slower," she said.

"What?" Scott felt a shock almost as great as the bout of cold. He pushed his way into the room. "You mean you know what's happening to me? Why didn't you—"

He stopped abruptly when he realized that there were other people in the room.

Drake stood a few paces behind Chloe. Beside him stood a tall man with a shock of iron gray hair who Scott didn't know.

Behind them both a woman lay sprawled on the floor. There was a length of rope around her wrists, and a hood of black cloth stretched over her head.

"What's going on?" Scott asked. He stepped toward the bound woman. "Who is that?"

Chloe closed the door. "You might as well show him," she said. "He doesn't have long."

Drake nodded and knelt down beside the woman. With a swift jerk of his hand he pulled away the hood, revealing a round face with a sprinkle of freckles.

Scott fell to his knees. "Dee," he gasped.

It was morning as the van rolled down off the last hills of northern Missouri and headed out onto the Great Plains.

Harley yawned and rubbed her eyes. She had been driving most of the night while Kenyon slept in the passenger seat. They had traveled almost five hundred miles west since the phone call, but there was still a lot of ground to cover, and the fuel gauge was once again hovering near empty. As an exit came up on the right she steered the big van up the ramp and circled down the service road to pull up to a gas pump.

Kenyon woke as she was opening the door. His black hair had been mashed down by sleep, and beard stubble darkened his chin. Harley liked the look. With his hair mussed and his clothes wrinkled, Kenyon looked a little less perfect and a little more human.

"Where are we?" he asked.

"Iowa," said Harley. "A couple hours away from South Dakota." She stretched her back and shook out her tangled hair. "You feel like driving for a while?"

Kenyon nodded. "It would be easier if we knew where we were driving *to.*"

"Noah said the badlands," said Harley.

Kenyon rolled his eyes. "It was a dream, Harley."

"It was more than a dream."

"Even if it was, what makes you think it had anything

122

to do with Dee?" Kenyon circled the van and pulled the handle down from the gas pump. "Besides, every state west of the Mississippi must have a place called the badlands."

"But only one of them is a national monument." Harley leaned against the side of the van and looked west across the flat, treeless landscape. "It has to be the South Dakota badlands."

"It doesn't have to be," Kenyon replied. "It doesn't have to mean anything. You're only guessing."

A spark of anger drove away the sleepiness that Harley had been feeling. "That's right," she said. "I *am* guessing. Some of us like to hope something will work out every now and then. Some of us have learned to trust our feelings."

"It's a bad habit." Kenyon pumped the last of the gas and swiped his credit card through the pump.

Harley fumed, but she was too tired to think of a good response.

She climbed up into the passenger seat and pulled the door closed. It would take them another ten hours of driving to reach the borders of Badlands National Monument. And even then they would have a big area to cover.

She wished she had a copy of the message that had come to the police station. The note had showed up at the station addressed to Kathleen Vincent. It had been pure luck that Dee had been at the station when the note arrived—pure bad luck. As soon as Dee saw the contents of the note she had run from the police station, taking the note with her. By the time Chief Janes got to the station, Dee had cleaned out her bank account and disappeared from Stone Harbor.

Harley stared out at the long flat stretch of road as Kenyon steered the van back onto the highway and turned up the interstate to the northwest. Ten more hours. She hated to admit it, but she didn't feel completely certain that Noah's parting words had anything to do with Dee. Harley sighed. It had to be right. If it wasn't, then they really were lost.

Tired as she was, Harley wasn't sure she could sleep. She closed her eyes, hoping to find the light that came when Noah visited her in her dreams, but all she saw was the back of her eyelids.

There was a loud bang, and the van jerked hard to the right. Harley sat up and looked around. "What was that?"

"I think it's a flat tire," said Kenyon. He slowed the van and started easing onto the shoulder of the highway. "We'll have to change it."

Harley looked out her window and realized that she must have dozed for at least a little while. They had moved into an area where immense cornfields stretched into the distance on either side of the highway. The interstate around them was all but empty. There was only a big semitruck a half mile ahead and a dark blue sedan a hundred yards behind.

Kenyon eased the van completely onto the shoulder of the interstate and pressed the brakes. As the vehicle slowed, Harley could hear the thump-thump-thump of the flapping tire.

Harley suddenly felt a tingling sensation across her skin and a tightening in her stomach. "Something's wrong," she said immediately.

"Of course something's wrong," said Kenyon. "It's a flat tire. You can hear it for yourself."

"No," Harley replied with a violent shake of her head. "That's not it." She glanced into the side mirror again and saw that the blue sedan was still behind them. It was slowing, keeping pace with the van.

"Go!" shouted Harley. "Speed up!"

Kenyon looked at her as if she were crazy. "I can't speed up. We've got a flat."

"I know we have a flat," Harley shot back. She pointed over her shoulder at the sedan. "They gave us the flat. That's Unit 17 back there."

Harley had to give Kenyon credit—he didn't stop to ask Harley how or why she thought the people behind them were agents. He just hit the gas.

The van swayed on its flat tire and skidded to the right. There was a thump, and Harley saw the tattered remains of the tire go flying out behind them. A screech rose as the metal rim of the wheel scraped over the road. The blue sedan fell back, then began to close in again.

"We can't do this for long!" Kenyon shouted over the screaming of the bare wheel. "See if you can get into the steel chest behind your seat."

"What's in it?" asked Harley.

"An XM-22 Stoner assault rifle and six hundred rounds of ammunition," Kenyon replied. "If you can get to it, I think it might be enough to keep Unit 17 from following too close."

Harley pulled around in her seat belt harness and stretched out her arms to the shiny metal box. She threw open the lid. But just as she reached for the stubby rifle inside, the van jerked and took a sharp skid to the left.

"They got the other tire!" Kenyon shouted. "Hold on!"

The van fishtailed left, then right, then left again. Harley twisted around in her harness and managed to face forward just in time for the van to leave the road. With a heavy thud the big vehicle barreled down the slope at the side of the highway, smashed through a wire fence, and blasted on into the corn.

Green stalks smashed against the front of the van and piled up on the windshield. Pale sap ran across the glass in streams.

Harley glanced in the mirror. "You can stop now!" she shouted. "They're not following."

"Don't you think I'm *trying* to stop?" Kenyon cried in response. He slammed both feet on the brake pedal and pressed so hard that he lifted himself out of his seat, but the van kept plowing on. "One of their shots must have cut a brake line!"

"What about the gears?" Harley suggested. "Try throwing it into low gear!"

Kenyon reached for the shifter, but he never got the chance to follow her advice. One moment they were chopping through the corn, the next Harley's stomach flew into her throat as the van burst into the air above a drainage ditch. For a second Harley thought the van might actually clear the ditch, but gravity didn't forget the heavy vehicle. The nose of the van dipped down, and a muddy bank rushed up to meet them at a speed that left Harley screaming.

Air bags exploded into the van with bangs as loud as any gun. Harley was slammed back against her seat as the off-white bag folded around her. There was a final crash. A groan of stressed metal. Then silence.

Spots of dark and light swam across Harley's vision, and she felt an iron weight of sleep pressing down. She shook it off and fumbled at the air bag with numb hands. "Kenyon?" she called. "Are you all right?" There was no answer from the left side of the van.

Harley forced open her door and squeezed her head out of the vehicle. The front of the van was buried three feet into a muddy earthen bank.

Harley hung there above the mud, listening to the cooling car. Her eyes fluttered closed, and a thick cloud of sleep began to descend. She had never felt so tired in her life.

A car door slammed in the distance. At once Harley was completely awake. *Unit 17.*

With a shove of her long legs Harley pushed herself out the door and fell on her hands and knees in the mud. She got quickly to her feet and hurried around to the other side of the van.

The driver's side door was still closed. Harley grabbed the handle, braced her feet in the mud, and pulled. The door opened with a creak of twisted metal. The air bag on the driver's side had started to deflate, but Kenyon sat with his head thrown back and his eyes closed. His usually olive skin was a pale, dusty shade. Harley reached for the buckle of his seat belt and popped it open. Kenyon sagged back in his seat.

"Kenyon!" Harley whispered fiercely. "Kenyon,

get up." She shook his shoulder, but Kenyon's head only swung loosely.

A needle of ice ran down Harley's spine. He's dead, she thought. Despite the air bags the crash had been tremendous. Kenyon might have broken his neck, or gotten busted up inside, or—

Kenyon groaned. His dark eyes fluttered open and then closed again.

"You're alive!" Harley said it louder than she wanted. She turned around and looked to see if the Unit 17 agents were close, but she could see nothing but the tall green stalks of corn and the ragged end of the path the van had cut through the grain. She leaned back toward Kenyon and spoke as softly as her fear and excitement would allow. "You have to get up. The Unit 17 agents are coming."

Kenyon muttered something, but his eyes remained closed.

Harley put both hands on his shoulders and shook him hard enough to knock his head against the back of the seat. "Get up!" she said. "We need to get moving."

"Moving?" Kenyon opened one eye and shook his head weakly. "Need to sleep," he mumbled.

Harley gave him another vigorous shake. "You've probably got a concussion, and if you go to sleep, you could go into a coma, but you won't get a chance because those freaks from Unit 17 are going to show up any second and kill both of us!" She drew in a deep breath and slapped Kenyon hard across the face.

Kenyon's dark eyes flew open. His hand shot up and caught Harley by the wrist. There was a muddy streak on his face from the impact of Harley's palm. "Don't ever do that again," he said in a deadly calm voice.

Harley jerked her hand free. "I won't if you'll just get up!"

The murderous look went out of Kenyon's eyes. He blinked and looked around him. "Where are we?"

"We're in the middle of a ditch, and we're about to get killed!"

An expression of great concentration tensed Kenyon's face. "I remember leaving Stone Harbor. . . ."

Harley was tempted to slap him again. "Oh, never mind. Just stay there a second."

She ran around to the back of the van. The motorcycle was splotched with mud, and there were corn shucks caught in the wheels, but it appeared to be unhurt. Harley glanced over her shoulder. There was still no sign of the Unit 17 agents. Working as quickly as she could, she unscrewed the clamps holding the bike into its iron cradle.

The Sportster was light for a motorcycle, but it was still a very heavy machine. Harley grunted with effort as she tried to pull the bike free from the cradle. Her feet slipped in the mud, and sweat trickled down her face.

"Over here," called a voice from the corn. "They went this way."

Harley put a foot against the back of the van and pulled until she was hanging in the air. The motorcycle shivered, shook, and came free from the rack with a clang of metal.

"This way!" shouted the voice in the corn. "I think I see them."

Harley pushed the motorcycle around to the side of the van. Kenyon was sitting on the lip of the open door. He looked up as Harley approached. "Something happened at a restaurant," he said.

"Something terrible," Harley agreed. "Now get on the motorcycle or something horrible will happen right here."

Kenyon rose to his feet and walked toward her. "Are we going for a ride?" His steps were slow and uncertain.

A growling, buzz saw whine rose up from the cornfield. Sparks flew from the top of the van as one of the Unit 17 agents fired his weapon. The glass at the back of the van imploded in a spray of tiny fragments. Chunks of gleaming metal snapped free from the motorcycle cradle and flew across the van to vanish in the cornfield.

"Get on!" Harley screamed. "Hurry!" She threw her leg over the bike and waited while Kenyon mounted with agonizing slowness. As soon as he was on board she hit the starter. The engine roared into life. "Hold on!" she called.

With a twist of the throttle Harley sent the motorcycle shooting out along the center of the ditch. As soon as she was clear of the van she heard the whine of the Unit 17 weapons. Cornstalks were cut off as cleanly as if they had been hit by a sickle. Water and mud geysered from the bottom of the ditch as the blasts came nearer.

Kenyon suddenly slumped to the right. The bike skidded around and through a plume of brown water as Harley fought for control. "Are you hit?" she called over her shoulder.

"Hit?" Kenyon replied in a sleepy voice.

Harley reached back with one hand and grabbed the front of his shirt. "Sit up straight or we're going to wreck," she ordered. "Put your hands around my waist."

Kenyon's arms moved clumsily to comply.

"Now hold on tight!"

Harley pulled the throttle back full and snapped the handlebars to the right. The rear wheel spun madly and threw clots of mud high into the air, then the treads managed a grip on the bottom of the ditch and the motorcycle shot up the steep bank.

The fire from the Unit 17 agents followed them up the bank. One of the turn signals suddenly vanished from the side of the bike in a puff of pulverized metal. The end of the throttle control was torn off less than an inch from where Harley's hand gripped the rubber.

They cleared the bank and the ditch and started into the green maze of corn. Thick leaves slapped at Harley's face, and the rough edges cut into the skin of her neck and arms. She hunched down to avoid as much of the blows as she could, but a hundred yards into the corn her arms were already sliced with fresh lines of blood.

"Where are we?" Kenyon asked from behind her.

Harley almost snarled at the question, but the tone of Kenyon's voice seemed more alert. The fast and painful passage through the corn seemed to finally be waking him from his shocked doze. "We're running for our lives," she replied.

"What else is new?" asked Kenyon.

Dee Janes's face was almost as red as her hair. "You *knew* she was in Umbra?" Dee asked for the third time.

Scott looked at the ground and nodded. They were back in the room where Scott had been staying, but now it was more prison cell than bedroom. Through the night Dee had been tied to the bed while Scott was bound in the room's only chair. "Yes," he admitted. "I knew she was in Umbra."

Dee strained against the ropes that held her to the narrow wooden bed. For most of the night Dee had been unconscious. Scott had begun to worry that Dee might have slumped into a coma from which she would never wake up. But now that she was awake, he was starting to think it was a shame that Dee hadn't stayed asleep a few more hours.

"You knew she was involved with this organization of thousand-year-old witches who want to take over the world," Dee said slowly, "and you still left me behind and followed her across the country."

Scott shifted uncomfortably in his chair. "They're not witches."

Dee shrugged. "Yeah, right. I saw Billie, and I know what Harley told me about the Umbra base in Virginia. You call them what you want, but *witches* is close enough for me."

"They're not like that here." Scott stretched his

bound arms to the limits of the chains and rubbed his tired eyes. "I think we've covered this enough."

Dee lay back against the hard bed. "I just want to make sure I really understand what's going on," she said. "I think I understand what you did. What I don't understand is why I was such an idiot that I rushed all the way across the country to save you from your new girlfriend."

"Chloe is not my girlfriend," Scott replied quickly. But the memory of the kiss they had shared sent an arrow of guilt into his heart. He held up his own hands and rattled the dark chains around his wrists. "If she was, would I have been locked up in here all night just like you?"

"I didn't say she was a very *good* girlfriend," said Dee. She closed her brown eyes. Her voice dropped to a whisper and lost its usual sarcastic edge. "Why did you come, Scott? The truth."

Scott opened his mouth to explain and closed it again. He shook his head. "The truth is I went with her because . . . because she's Chloe."

To Scott's surprise, the answer seemed to satisfy Dee. The expression on her round face softened. "You looked for her a long time. Ever since you were a kid."

"Yes." Scott nodded. The back of his throat burned, and he was embarrassed to realize that his eyes were brimming with tears.

Dee opened her eyes and looked at him over her knees. "She meant everything to you once. So when you got the chance to be with her again, you gave up everything. Including me."

"Yes," Scott whispered.

"But she's not Chloe, is she?" Scott started to protest, but Dee went on quickly. "Oh, I know she's the same girl, but she's not really the same *person,* is she?"

This time Scott couldn't manage to speak. He could only nod.

Dee sighed. "You know, I was worried that you were in love with Chloe, but you're not in love with her at all."

The words surprised Scott. "I'm not?" he choked out.

"No," Dee replied. "You were happy with me, but you left, anyway. It's not love—it's a mental illness."

"Just because I missed Chloe doesn't mean I'm crazy," said Scott.

"You didn't *miss* her, Scott. You're *obsessed* with her."

"I'm not!" Scott protested. "She's the closest person in the world to me. She's the only one I have!"

Dee's lips curled in anger. "Listen to yourself," she said. "You're talking about someone you hadn't seen in more than five years. What about me, Scott? What about Kenyon and Harley? Aren't we your friends?"

"Not like Chloe. She's—"

"She's nothing!" Dee shouted. "A little girl named Chloe was a friend of a little boy named Scott. But you're not that lonely kid, and she's not that little girl. Give it up, Scott."

Dee's words burned in Scott's mind. Twice he opened his mouth to reply, but both times the words slipped away from him before he could speak. An image of Chloe floated through his mind—the twelve-year-old Chloe he had known from the orphanage. Somehow the image seemed faded and tattered, like an old photograph left too long in the sun.

"She . . . she's not the same," he admitted. But there was another set of images in Scott's mind. He remembered the kiss that he and Chloe had shared and the incredible feelings that he had felt at her touch. Even now he couldn't deny the desire he felt for her. He had to be with Chloe. *Had to.* It was a law as important as breathing. "But she's still Chloe."

Dee scooted around on the bed. She nodded toward the window. "This is quite the little plantation your pal has going here. What are all these people up to?"

Scott wasn't sure where Dee was going with the question, but he was glad to talk about something else besides his relationship with Chloe. "There's this ceremony," he explained. "They've been trying to generate a white sphere."

"A sphere?" Dee frowned, and lines creased the smooth skin of her forehead. "You mean like the one Unit 17 was building? Like the sphere that Noah went into?"

Scott nodded. "Umbra can make one just by using their minds. Or at least they almost can. They were a little short of power, so I built a machine to—"

"You did what?" Dee asked. Her brown eyes were wide. "You built a machine to help Umbra?"

Scott started to nod, but then the impact of the statement sank in. He had been thinking only of Chloe. He had wanted to be with her, and he had wanted to please her. But he had built something that would give Umbra a terrible advantage. He lowered his face and looked at the floor. "I think . . . I think they'll be able to make a sphere with the machine I built them."

Dee gave out a deep sigh. "I don't suppose you know what they plan to do with the sphere if they get it going?"

Someone must have told him Umbra's plans for the white sphere, but now that he concentrated on the idea, he couldn't remember a thing. "No, I don't guess I know."

"Wonderful," said Dee. "Your old pal Chloe and her bunch of Froot Loops are about to get their hands on the most powerful force in the world, and we don't know what they're going to do with it." She shook her head. "Remind me to slap you good as soon as someone unties me."

They sat in silence for a few moments.

"Now what?" Dee asked finally. "Do you have any idea what she plans on doing with us?"

Scott swallowed hard. "There's going to be a ceremony," he said. "I think she'll want us there."

"They're going to make the sphere tonight?"

"I think—" Scott stopped as a new bout of shivering came over him. The cold had shaken him several times in the night, and each time it seemed to be stronger. This time he trembled so violently that the chains rattled around his wrists.

"What's wrong with you?" Dee asked. Her brown eyes narrowed. "Are you sick?"

Scott raised his head to look at her. As he did, his vision abruptly shifted into the strange spread of grays that had overcome him once before, but this time far more changed than just the colors. The walls of the room were made of light-colored wood. In an instant they wavered and became heaps of skulls stacked one upon the other. Scott could see the empty nostrils, the dark void of the eyes, and the grinning bare teeth set in broken jaws. The bed was built from longer bones—arched ribs and rounded sections of limbs. On the bed sat a complete skeleton with dry strands of mummified tendons still clinging to the joints. Ratted, moldering rags gave the skeleton a nightmare wardrobe, and a few twisted tufts of hair clung stubbornly to the skull.

The skeleton's jaw swung open. "Scott?" it asked in Dee Jane's voice. A black beetle crawled out of its mouth and clung to the rotted stump of a tooth. "What's wrong?"

Scott let out a wordless scream. He closed his eyes, but he could still see the skeleton seated on its bed of bones. With a rattle of chains he pulled his hands forward and clamped them over his eyes. Even then he couldn't block the grisly sight. His hands seemed as transparent as fog. "They've done something to me!" he cried.

The door to the room suddenly opened. "No," said Chloe. "You've done it to yourself."

Scott swung toward her, expecting to see another animated skeleton. The room around her remained a nightmare of bones and death, but Chloe was as beautiful as ever. In the world of gray, she was the only spot of color. Her hair was still deep and curling gold. Her skin was smooth and radiant. She walked gracefully into the room with her purple robe shifting around her body.

The skeleton on the bed stirred, and flakes of dried skin sifted down. The jaw swung again, like some horrible toy in a novelty shop. "Get tired of stirring your cauldron?" the awful figure with Dee's voice said. "Run out of bat wings?"

Chloe laughed musically. "I can see why he liked you." She glanced over at Scott, and the corners of her mouth turned up in a grin. "But right now I don't think he finds you too attractive." She stepped over to Scott, put her hand under his chin, and lifted his face. "You want to tell her what you see, Scott?"

Scott struggled. "Make it stop," he begged.

Chloe's fingers gently caressed his cheek. "I wish I could," she said in a soothing voice. "This really isn't what I wanted." Even as the tips of her fingers ran smoothly along Scott's face, Chloe continued to grin. The grin still reminded Scott of the mischievous grin of the Chloe he had grown up with, but now he could see what he had missed before. It was a cold grin, a mean grin. Despite her sympathetic words Chloe was enjoying the situation.

Then abruptly the horrible visions vanished. The wall of skulls became smooth, clean paneling. The bed returned to simple wood and cloth. And Dee was just Dee.

Scott blinked. "I'm better," he said with relief. "Everything's back to normal."

"Who's to say what's normal?" Chloe replied. She stepped away and stood with her hands clasped beneath the sleeves of her robe. "The world is nothing but a dream."

"What I saw was no dream!" Scott rubbed his shackled hands across his eyes and almost sobbed in relief when he saw that his own flesh was again solid. "This is a nightmare."

"Don't worry," said Chloe. "You won't have long before the change is complete. Then your reality will be constant again."

"What change?" Scott asked. "What's happening to me?"

"I think you know," said Chloe.

Far down in Scott's guts he felt a wavering doubt. "I don't know," he insisted. He opened his eyes and stared up into Chloe's luminous face. "Tell me."

Another hard smile turned up the corners of Chloe's mouth. "You've always been so good at lying to yourself," she said.

"Hey," Dee called from across the room. "If you don't want to tell him, tell me. I promise I have absolutely no idea what's going on."

Chloe's smile faded. She glanced at Dee with a cool expression. "I doubt you're as ignorant as you pretend. Otherwise you never would have found us."

"Oh, I'm stupider than you think," said Dee. "Try me."

Chloe cast a quick look at Scott. "Scott took part in one of our ceremonies and opened himself to the circle of power. It's had a very poor effect on him."

Scott remembered the freedom and joy he had felt during the ceremony—and that the first bout of cold had come over him that night. "But you *asked* me to go to the ceremony."

Chloe gave a graceful shrug. "I had no intention of this happening. According to the information we gained from Legion, you shouldn't have been capable of channeling enough power to initiate the change."

"What information from Legion?"

Chloe faced him and shook back her thick wavy hair. "Oh, didn't I tell you? We have the complete Legion records on your design." She reached out again and put her hand against his face, but this time her grip was hard. Her fingers dug into the flesh of his cheek with painful force. "You were designed as my companion. You were supposed to grow up and replace the Legion guards who watched me every minute of my life."

Scott remembered the man who had watched them at the orphanage and who had come to him in Stone Harbor still looking for Chloe. "You mean I'm like Gunter Rhinehardt?" he asked. He had to fight to get the words out with Chloe's fingers pressing hard into his face.

"Exactly." Chloe nodded. She leaned down and brought her face so close to Scott that for a moment he thought she was going to give him another kiss. "I won't be made a prisoner, Scott." Her voice was a soft hiss. "I fought to get away from the orphanage, and I'm not going to be made a nice little pet. Not by Rhinehardt, not by Legion, not by you."

"I didn't want to make you a prisoner," Scott replied. "I only wanted to be with you."

Chloe shoved back his head and stood. "You think you care about me, but it's your genes talking. Your behavior was coded into your chromosomes."

Scott felt the images in his mind shifting and thinning. The face of his childhood friend faded and ran like watercolors in the rain. "It was more than that," he said weakly.

"Was it?" Chloe shook her head. "Think back, Scott. Were we alike as kids? Did we have any interests in common?"

"No, but . . ."

"No!" For the first time Chloe's expression slipped into an angry sneer. "We were friends only because we were *built* that way. If it hadn't been for Legion, we would never even have noticed each other."

Scott looked at her in shock. In one part of his mind he knew that there was some truth in everything Chloe said, but in his heart he couldn't admit that their friendship had been brewed up in some beaker. "I cared about you," he whispered.

Chloe stood still for a moment, then she suddenly crossed the room in three quick strides. She reached out, wrapped her hands around Dee Janes's throat, and squeezed with such force that Dee's eyes bulged.

"Stop!" screamed Scott. "What are you doing?"

"I'm showing you the truth," said Chloe. Dee tried desperately to fight back, but with her arms and legs tied she could do little more than thrash against the wooden bed. Chloe held her grip. The skin around her fingers grew bone white, and Dee's face began to turn dark.

Scott surged forward. The chains around his arms crashed and snapped taut, but he couldn't get close to Dee. "You're killing her!"

"Yes," Chloe said calmly. "I know this girl is your friend, and I'm killing her." Dee's struggles began to weaken. Her hands sagged against the ropes that held them.

"Why?" Scott cried. "Why are you doing this?"

Chloe glanced at him through the curtain of her golden hair. "If I let you go, would you stop me?"

"Yes!"

"Even if you had to fight me?" asked Chloe. "If

141

you had to hit me to keep me from killing your friend, would you hurt me?"

"I . . . I . . ." Scott wanted to say yes, but at the thought of doing anything to hurt Chloe, a door slammed shut in his mind. "No," he admitted. He felt a disgust with himself, but it was the truth. The idea of hurting Chloe was utterly alien. "I wouldn't hurt you."

Chloe released her stranglehold on Dee's throat. Dee fell forward with her eyes closed. The pale skin of her neck began to blossom with angry bruises.

"You see," said Chloe. "You're made as my protector. You can't hurt me even if it means saving the life of your friend."

Scott felt painfully, horribly ashamed. He couldn't hurt Chloe, but in that moment he would have cheerfully hurt himself. He looked over at Dee's limp body. "Is she dead?"

"No," said Chloe. She stepped away from Dee and adjusted her robe. "Tonight we'll hold the ceremony. Using your machine, we'll have no trouble opening the gateway and keeping it open."

"Gateway?" Scott repeated in confusion. "You mean the sphere?"

"It's a sphere in form," said Chloe, "but for us it is a gateway."

Scott wasn't sure what she was talking about. He shook his head. "It doesn't matter what you call it— you won't get the sphere tonight."

Chloe smiled in amusement. "Oh? And why not?"

"Because my machine is only half finished." Scott

tried to summon up as much dignity as he had left and looked straight into Chloe's blue eyes. "I may not be able to hurt you, but you can't make me finish the machine."

The remark brought a peal of musical laughter. "The machine is finished already."

Scott frowned. "But how?"

"You were very good in telling Drake everything about your design," said Chloe. "He and Alice have been up most of the night completing the device." She paused and smiled broadly. "By the way, congratulations. It works just as you said it would."

A feeling of absolute despair settled over Scott. "What happens now?" he asked.

Chloe walked to the door of the room and put her hand on the brass latch. "Now we wait for sunset," she said. "When it comes, we will take you and your friend Dee down to the ceremony grounds. We all have our parts to play in tonight's event."

"Why take Dee?" Scott asked. "She doesn't have any special powers."

"She's not going to increase the power of the circle," said Chloe. "You've already seen to it that we'll have more than we need." She pulled open the door and flashed a final smile. "Your friend is going to be there in case any of the ancient ones get hungry."

THIRTEEN

Harley dangled her feet over the edge of the cliff and stared at the jagged, unearthly landscape of the South Dakota badlands.

A clatter of tumbling rocks made Harley turn around quickly. She was relieved to see that it was only Kenyon making his way along the path from the place where they had parked the Sportster. "Are you feeling better?" she asked.

Kenyon nodded absently. It had taken him hours to throw off the confusion after the accident in the cornfield, and Harley had begun to worry that he might be seriously injured. But as the day rolled on he seemed to get his thoughts in order. If Kenyon had a concussion, it didn't seem to be serious.

He sat down on a slab of fractured gray shale a dozen feet from Harley, pulled out his billfold, and began sorting through the contents. "It has to be the credit card," he said.

"Isn't this a strange time to be worrying about your finances?" asked Harley. She wondered if his skull was fractured after all.

"I'm not worried about my credit limit," Kenyon replied. He pulled out the gold plastic rectangle of a credit card and waved it through the air. "I'm thinking about Unit 17."

Harley frowned for a moment, then nodded as

she remembered Kenyon using the card to buy gas shortly before Unit 17 attacked them on the highway. "If they're keyed into the credit network, then that would explain how they managed to find us in the middle of nowhere."

With a flick of his wrist Kenyon sailed the suspect card past Harley's shoulder and out over the lip of the sharp cliff. The little piece of plastic caught the sun in a flash of golden light, then vanished into a pile of boulders.

Kenyon packed the rest of his cards and cash back into his billfold and shoved it into his jeans pocket. "We're going to have to be careful from here on out. We can't afford to use any sort of identification. If we buy anything, we need to use cash."

Harley spread her arms to take in the valley of ragged stones and stunted trees. "I don't think we need to worry about it," she said. "There's nothing out here to buy."

They had traveled all day along gravel back roads. Twice they had dared short stints on larger highways, but both Harley and Kenyon had been nervous about being spotted. Taking turns driving the motorcycle, they had reached the badlands early in the afternoon. Since then they had skirted the national monument area, given a quick look to part of the huge Lakota Sioux reservation, and wandered through small towns and past trading posts. There was no sign of Dee, Scott, or anything unusual.

Kenyon stood up off his rock and walked closer to Harley. He glanced down and scowled. "You shouldn't sit so close to the edge."

Harley noticed the dark look in his eyes. "What's wrong?" she asked. "Afraid of heights?"

"No," said Kenyon. "I'm afraid of falling three or four hundred feet and spreading out over rock like jam on toast. I'm even more afraid of *you* falling three or four hundred feet." He reached out his hand. "How about moving away from the edge?"

Harley suspected there was a compliment somewhere in Kenyon's words, but she felt too road weary to work it out. She kicked her heels against the cliff face, sending a stream of gravel-size stones rolling down, then she reached up and let Kenyon pull her back from the lip of the drop.

"What now?" she asked. "Where do we go?"

Kenyon shrugged. "You tell me. I thought you were the one with the mystical visions."

Harley ran her fingers through her wind-tangled hair. She was half tempted to suggest they go straight to a motel. A shower and a hot meal sounded wonderful. But she couldn't stand the idea of leaving Dee somewhere alone in this unearthly place. "My mystical visions didn't give precise directions," she said. Harley glanced over her shoulder at the vast spread of empty landscape. "It would be easier if we had some idea of what to look for."

"I can tell you that," said a voice from behind a split boulder.

Harley stepped back in surprise. Her left foot slipped off into space and she swung her arms madly to keep from falling down the cliff. Kenyon reached out to steady her.

"Thanks," Harley said quickly. She looked toward the boulder where the voice had spoken. "Who's there?" she asked.

Lydia Abel stepped out from behind the stones. As usual, she was dressed far too elegantly for the situation in a peach-colored silk dress that left her shoulders bare and clung to her figure. A strand of glistening pearls hung around her neck, and she wore heels that made her almost as tall as Harley. "I thought you two would be lost by now." She paused, and her red lips turned up in a mocking smile. "Whatever would you do without my help?"

Harley shook her head. She was too tired to be really shocked, but Abel's words managed to bring up a warm edge of anger. "How did you get here?" she asked.

"I came by plane," the woman replied. "And by . . . other means of transport. I've been in the area for hours, just waiting for you to show up." She walked across to Kenyon and stared critically at his face. "It looks like you two have had a rough trip."

Kenyon returned her stare with a hard, flat look. "We're fine," he said.

Abel smiled. "Yes. You certainly are." She shook back her head so that the dark fall of her hair brushed against her bare shoulders. "Do be careful. I'd hate to think anything might happen that would spoil your classic profile, Mr. Moor."

The woman's outrageous flirting only increased Harley's irritation. "How did you know we'd be here?" she demanded.

Abel cut her blue eyes to the side and glanced at Harley without turning her head. "I followed you."

"But how?"

"I used the same system that allowed Unit 17 to track your motions," replied Abel.

Kenyon spoke up. "How could the credit network lead you here? We haven't used a card in five hundred miles."

The agent smiled. "The credit network has nothing to do with it. Speaking of which—" Abel reached down and seemed to draw something out of midair. When she raised her hand, Harley saw that she was holding the gold credit card that Kenyon had tossed away. "I believe you dropped this."

Kenyon's dark eyes widened. He glanced at Abel, turned to look at the cliff, then turned back to the woman in the clinging dress. "But how—"

Abel laughed. "I believe I've managed to surprise the unshakable Mr. Moor. How wonderful."

Kenyon's face settled back into its usual scowl. He tugged the card away from the agent's fingers and shoved it quickly into his jeans. "If it's not the card, then how did Unit 17 know where to find us?"

Lydia Abel extended the index finger on her right hand and made a circling motion in the air. "It's your wheels."

"What about the wheels?" asked Harley.

"Unit 17 planted microprobes on them," said Abel. "They probably scattered the sensors along the road leading into the beach house and infected your vehicle when you drove up."

"What do these microprobes do?"

Abel brushed her hand along the top of the stone where Kenyon had been sitting, looked as if she was going to sit down herself, then frowned and remained standing. "The micros are pretty dumb," she said, "but they're capable of reporting some basic information—including their position. Unit 17 has listening posts scattered across the country. Every time you came close to one, Unit 17 got an update on your location."

Harley thought about the information for a moment. "That explains how Unit 17 caught us, but it doesn't explain how you got here."

Abel waved her hand languidly through the air. "Such useless questions," she said. "Don't you have something more important to ask me?"

"Yes," Kenyon replied quickly. "Where are Scott and Dee?"

The woman looked at Kenyon with a warm expression. "Bravo. I knew I could count on you to come straight to the point." She ran her hand across Kenyon's chest and up to a tear in his sweater. For a moment Harley could have sworn she saw something spread across Kenyon's chest, something that glittered like gold dust, but in the blink of an eye it was gone.

Abel's fingers traced the muscles at Kenyon's shoulder. "You really did have a hard knock, didn't you?"

Kenyon grabbed the woman by the wrist. "Just tell me where to find Scott and Dee," he said in a low voice.

Agent Abel's face went cold. "Careful, Mr. Moor. There are no soft sand dunes here. If you force me to correct your rudeness again, your friend Harley will have to find someone else to share the seat on her little motorcycle."

For a moment Harley was afraid that Kenyon was going to try to fight. She was glad to see that Kenyon was resisting Abel's advances, but she didn't want it to go any further. Even though Kenyon was a good six inches taller and nearly twice the weight of the slender woman, Harley had no doubt who would win the contest. She hoped Kenyon didn't allow anger to get the better of his brain.

"Let her go," Harley urged. "It's not worth fighting."

After another moment of hesitation Kenyon released Abel's hand. "All right."

"Well," said Abel. "It's nice to see that you do follow instructions." She tilted her head to the right so that her smooth hair spilled over her shoulder on that side. "I wonder how you would be at following my directions?"

A fresh burst of anger drove away Harley's exhaustion. "I'm tired of the games," she said bluntly. "Tell us where to find Dee."

"Certainly," replied the agent. She raised an elegant arm and pointed to the north. "You'll find her at a place called the Daystar Cooperative. It's just over twenty miles from here."

"What's this Daystar Cooperative?"

"It's an Umbra cover operation."

"Umbra?" Harley was surprised. She knew Legion was involved, and Unit 17 had followed them across the country. Now Umbra was also in the picture. Whatever was going on, it seemed that all three of the major secret organizations had a part.

Abel raised a hand to her mouth in mock surprise. "Oh, didn't I tell you? Scott's childhood chum, Chloe, is an Umbra bigwig these days. She brought him home, and Ms. Janes followed. Now they're all nice and snug at Daystar."

"Chloe's part of Umbra?" The idea left Harley stunned. She thought of the horrible things she had seen in Umbra's underground lair outside Washington, D.C., and of the monstrous power held by the woman-thing that called itself Billie. Harley had thought killing Billie might be the end of Umbra, but already Dee and Scott had fallen into the power of the dark society.

"What's this Daystar place like?" Kenyon asked. "How do we get Scott and Dee out?"

Abel shrugged. "You'll have to answer those questions yourself," she said. "I've already told you more than I should." She gave Kenyon a last appraising look, then turned away and started walking up the slope.

"Wait!" Harley called.

Abel stopped and spoke with her back to Harley. "I've already answered all the questions I can, Ms. Davisidaro."

"Just one more," said Harley. "Why?"

The agent turned around slowly. "Why?" She raised one thin eyebrow. "What sort of question is that?"

"Why?" Harley repeated. "You helped us avoid Unit 17 back in Stone Harbor, and now you're helping us find Scott and Dee. Why?"

Abel gave a sly smile. "Would you believe I did it out of the goodness of my heart?"

Harley shook her head. "I'm not even sure you have a heart."

"Ouch." Abel clasped her hands in front of her chest. "You wound me, Ms. Davisidaro." She spun on her high heels and stalked quickly away. In a few seconds she was gone.

Kenyon walked to Harley's side. "What now? Do we go to this Daystar place?"

Harley shrugged. "I guess we have to."

They walked back up the rough trail to where the Sportster sat amid a tight cluster of sagebrush. Harley once again took the controls and Kenyon held on to her waist as they drove off in the direction Abel had indicated. Fifteen minutes later they were outside a gate marked by a large white sign:

DAYSTAR COOPERATIVE
AN ENLIGHTENED FARMING COMMUNITY

Beside the gate was a smaller sign that provided more details on Daystar. It was filled with terms like "cooperation," "peaceful," and "natural." When Harley considered what she knew of Umbra, the sign almost made her laugh.

"What do you think?" she asked Kenyon. "Do we drive right in and ask to talk to the person in charge?"

"Maybe," Kenyon replied. He sat on the back of the motorcycle for a moment and rubbed the shadow of beard that days on the run had built along the square angle of his jaw. "I wish we had more weapons. All we have is my pistol."

"I was a little busy back at the van," Harley replied,

slightly irritated by his statement. "I didn't have much time to search for your weapons."

Kenyon nodded. "Let's look around and see if we can get a better idea of what we're facing before we go in."

Harley twisted the throttle on the bike and sent them moving along the road. A half mile farther on they came across the faint trace of an old Jeep trail among the sage and buffalo grass. Harley turned off the road and followed the trail to a pair of small buttes that rose above the surrounding terrain.

"Let's go up there," said Kenyon. "We should get a pretty good view from the top."

The sides of the butte were too steep for the motorcycle. They left the bike at the base and struggled upward. Harley grabbed at roots and clumps of grass as she pulled herself up. The butte was only a hundred feet tall, but climbing it was slow work. By the time they cleared the lip and stepped onto the flat cap of the rock tower, the sky was already turning purple with the approach of sunset.

The Daystar Cooperative lay sprawled out below them. Harley could see a dozen smaller buildings set in a loose circle around a larger central structure. A strange vehicle was parked near the center of the compound, and the slender form of a radio tower peeked up along one edge. As far as she could see, there was neither a single light nor a person in the whole place.

"What now?" she asked.

Kenyon moved cautiously up to stand beside her. "We can either go on in or we can wait here for something to happen, something that gives us an idea of what we're facing. We don't know if there are three people in there or thirty."

Harley was about to ask another question when a noise echoed up from the Daystar compound. She looked down to see people spilling from every building. The distance made them appear to be the size of ants, but it did nothing to hide the numbers. "It looks more like three hundred people in there."

Kenyon nodded. "Close to it."

"Okay, now that we know, what do we do next?"

Kenyon took his black pistol from his jacket, pulled back the action, then let it close with a solid metallic click. "Now we go get Scott and Dee."

Scott suffered through two more bouts of the cold before sunset.

The first was no more than a bad set of shivers, but the second sent Scott back into the land of bones. The horrible visions lasted longer this time, and they didn't stop with just sight. The chains around his hands were transformed into vast, powerful serpents. Their dry scales scraped over his wrists and hissed softly as the coils rubbed together. An odor of mold and rot filled the air. No matter what Scott did, he couldn't block one of the terrible sensations.

When the world finally returned to normal, Scott found his chains covered over in frost and his clothing damp. It was another strange new symptom, but Scott was so glad the fit was over that he didn't care.

The windows were colored with twilight when the door suddenly swung open and Chloe came into the room. "Time to leave," she said brightly. She had the hood of her purple robe raised around her face, but even from the shadows Scott could see the excitement in her eyes.

"Dee's still not awake," he said. "I think you really hurt her."

Chloe walked over to Dee and prodded her with a finger as if she were poking something unpleasant. "That's too bad." She shoved her hand into Dee's short auburn hair and lifted her head. Dee's eyes were closed, and her mouth hung open. The marks of Chloe's fingers were still clearly visible as dark bruises on Dee's throat. "It would be nicer if she was awake, but the ancient ones aren't that picky about their snacks."

"What do you mean, 'snacks'?" asked Scott. "And who are these ancient ones?"

Chloe made smacking sounds with her lips and moved her mouth as if she were chewing. "You'll find out soon enough," she said.

Two more robed figures stepped into the room. Their faces were hidden deep within their cowls. "Take them to the canyon," Chloe instructed. "Make sure they have a good view."

The robed men nodded. One of them walked to Dee and began to loosen the ropes that held her to the narrow bed. The second man approached Scott.

As he drew close, Scott felt a wave of cold. For a moment he thought he was having another round of the strange illness, then he realized that the cold was coming from the robed figure. Covered hands reached up and grasped the chains holding Scott's wrists. Immediately the metal links grew so cold that they burned Scott's flesh. He pulled away and stared into the darkness beneath the hood.

"What are you?" he gasped.

The figure in the robe snapped the chains like brittle candy. "You're kindred," it replied in an impossibly deep, echoing voice. It raised a hidden hand and brushed back the folds of its hood. There was no face. Instead Scott saw only a midnight black void in the shape of a human head. Thin trails of vapor rolled around the shoulders of the ghastly figure, and the air boiled with cold. Deep in the patch of darkness a spark of red gleamed.

Scott scrambled backward across the floor in an effort to get away from the thing in the robe. He had never seen anything like it before, but he had heard stories from Harley. "You're a shadow man," Scott whispered.

"I am a servant of the ancient one," the creature replied in its well-deep voice. It raised its arm and pointed a night-filled sleeve at Scott. "You must come."

Scott got shakily to his feet and pressed his back to the bare wall. He shook his head. "Stay away from me."

Across the room the second figure finished freeing Dee. Shadow hands slipped from the sleeves and lifted her from the bed. Dee moaned in her sleep.

"Let her go!" Scott shouted. He took a step toward Dee, but the first shadow man moved with unexpected speed to block his path.

"The Ipolex has spoken," it said. "You must come with us."

Scott watched helplessly as the other shadow man carried Dee from the room. He nodded. "All right, I'll come with you. Just don't hurt Dee."

The shadow man stepped aside and let Scott pass. He slipped past the dark figure and stumbled into the hall in time to see the other shadow man carrying Dee outside.

Scott hurried to catch up. He stepped through the door and stood blinking in the last crimson light of sunset. The shadow man holding Dee was a dozen feet ahead, walking slowly and steadily. A few other Daystar workers were out, some wearing their robes, others running to get dressed, but much of the compound appeared empty.

I could get away, Scott thought. If I ran and just kept running, I could be out of here.

The silent lines of Umbra members flowed toward the ceremony ground. None of them seemed to be paying attention to Scott. The shadow man holding Dee was a good five yards ahead. The one following Scott was at least that far behind.

He turned his head and quickly scanned the surrounding landscape. I could make it. I could go down the slope into the maze of canyons or run up to the highway and hope someone comes along.

He tensed the muscles of his legs and prepared to sprint, but at the last second he hesitated. Running away would mean leaving Dee behind.

Maybe I could go for help, Scott thought hopefully. I could get to a phone— His thoughts tumbled into confusion as he remembered that the nearest help he could count on was more than two thousand miles away. If someone was going to come back for Dee, it was going to take long hours. Maybe days.

Several times in the past Harley or her friend Noah had been captured by one of the secret organizations and held for long periods. Still—with the help of Kenyon, Scott, and Dee—they had managed eventually to get free. It was possible that if Scott got away, he could bring back others in a day or a week and extract Dee from the Daystar compound. But he didn't think so. Chloe expected something to happen at the ceremony tonight, and in his guts Scott thought she was right. Thanks to the machine he had built, this ceremony was going to be different.

I have to save Dee, he thought. All of this is my fault. But even as the thoughts crossed his mind, Scott felt the pull of his bond with Chloe. Burning with guilt and confusion, Scott fixed his eyes on the back of the shadow man that was carrying Dee and followed the creature toward the canyon.

Despite everything that had happened, Scott felt another dark thrill run through him as he recalled what would happen in the small canyon. *The ceremony.* Soon enough the chaos of singing and wild dancing would begin. No matter what horrors the strange ritual would bring, Scott couldn't deny the power and overwhelming emotions he had felt while taking part.

The marching crowd suddenly stopped at the crest of a low rise leading down into the box canyon where the ceremony was held. Scott looked up and saw Chloe standing at the top of the hill. With her were at least a dozen more of the shadow men, their midnight faces invisible within the hoods of their robes.

On the other side of the shadow men was a wooden cart loaded down with a strange device. The ten-foot span of a wire mesh satellite dish dominated the machine. Below that was a rank of lead-acid batteries and a snake's nest of cables. A computer was tucked in among the wires, beside a rough breadboard laced through with resistors and coils of copper. At the center of the contraption a bank of blue LED numbers glowed with cold fire.

Scott stared at the machine. He remembered the burst of creative joy he had experienced when he thought of how to amplify the power produced by the circle. It had seemed like a great trick—a wonderful experiment. Now that he was faced with the results of that experiment, he felt sick to think of what he had done.

Chloe looked down at Scott and smiled from the shadows of her hood. "What do you think of it?" she called to him. "Does it look like you expected?"

Scott started to nod, then caught himself and shook his head instead. He might not be able to hurt Chloe, but that didn't mean he was helpless. "No," he said. He reached up and ran a hand through his long hair. "Something's not right with the main breadboard." He stepped toward the machine. "Looks like it's wired wrong."

"Wrong?" Chloe frowned for a moment, then the cold grin returned to her face. "Zero!" she called sharply. "Stop him!"

One of the shadow men stepped forward and grabbed Scott by the arm. He struggled against its grip, but the thing seemed to be made from frozen steel. Cold seeped into his biceps like a breath of winter.

"Hold on to him for a moment, Zero," said Chloe. She raised her right hand and made a sharp gesture. At once Drake and Alice appeared from the crowd of Umbra followers.

The two technicians bowed their heads. "Yes, Ipolex?" they said together.

"My friend says there's something wrong with the machine," Chloe said smoothly. "What do you think?"

Alice tossed back her hood and glanced toward Scott. The expression in her eyes was far from friendly. "If there's anything wrong with it," she said, "it's because there was something wrong with the design. We built it exactly as he told us, and our test fit the predicted results."

Chloe nodded slowly. "So you think he's lying?"

"Yes," Alice replied bluntly. She gave Scott another withering look. "I think he wants to damage the machine."

Scott shook his head. "I only want to fix it."

"I see." Chloe looked at him for a moment, then turned her attention back to Alice. "Do you understand this machine?"

"I . . . no," Alice admitted. "I don't know how it works. Not exactly." She raised her small chin into the air. "But we built it right. I'll swear to it."

Chloe's eyes narrowed. "Be careful, Alice. Pride is dangerous."

Alice lowered her gaze to the ground. "Yes, Ipolex."

Chloe nodded. She glanced over at Scott, and her grin returned. "Nice try. Now come along, and we'll all get a chance to see your toy in action."

Scott looked at the machine and bit his lip. One loose wire or broken connection would be enough to cripple the device. If he could damage it badly enough, Drake and Alice might not be capable of making repairs. Scott made a lunge toward the machine, but the shadow man holding his arm jerked him back. "Keep the machine," Scott offered. "Just let us go."

"I don't think so," said Chloe. She gestured toward the canyon. "Take him down and hold him."

The shadow man dragged Scott back into line and forced him down the hill. As they grew close to the ceremony site he saw that rough pine timbers had been driven into the ground at the edge of the circle. Loops of rope dangled from the timber.

The robed figure carrying Dee dropped her into the dust in front of one of the wooden posts. In the dim light the bruises on her face seemed as dark as the faces of the shadow men.

"Be careful with her!" Scott shouted.

A rough shove sent him bouncing off the other piece of wood. "Stand still," rumbled the deep voice of the shadow man. It grabbed a length of rope and stretched the cord toward Scott. The hand on his arm released its grip as the dark creature moved to tie Scott to the wood.

Suddenly Dee rolled over on the ground. "Run!" she shouted. She jumped to her feet and pumped her short legs as she ran away from the post.

Before Scott had a chance to recover his wits, Dee had run past him. "Come on!" she shouted over her shoulder.

Scott shook off his paralysis and leaped forward. There was a momentary tug, and he felt cold, hard fingers close on the loose cloth of his shirt. Then the fabric gave way, and he was free. He dodged a grab from the other shadow man and raced after Dee.

She jumped over the small fire at the center of the

circle, swerved to avoid a cluster of Daystar members, and pounded on with dust spraying up around her feet. Scott tried to keep up. He was almost a foot taller than Dee, but he had a hard time matching her pace.

Instead of pushing through the crowd of Umbra members pouring down the hill, Dee turned left and ran straight toward the wall of the canyon. She put her foot into a crevice in the soft rock and began scrambling upward.

Scott glanced over his shoulder. The shadow men had been slow getting started, but they were coming like freight trains, their purple robes flapping madly around their midnight bodies. "Where are you going?" he shouted.

"Up!" Dee called in reply.

"Then what?"

"Who cares?" Dee glanced down at him for a second. "You have another plan?"

Scott shook his head. "No."

"Then climb!" Dee was already a good six feet off the canyon floor. Despite her small size she climbed with quick, confident movements.

Scott jumped at the cliff face beside Dee. The toes of his sneakers scuffed against the rock, and he slipped back to the ground. He jumped up again, and this time he managed to find a small ledge. He reached up with his long arms and scrambled for a handhold. He moved up a foot, then two.

Footsteps sounded behind them.

Scott didn't dare look around as he fought for every handhold. Dee found a finger-wide fracture in the stone and quickly gained another ten feet. "Hurry!" she shouted. She twisted around and reached down. "They're coming. Grab my hand!"

Trembling with effort, Scott stretched his fingers toward hers. Their hands locked together, and Scott shoved himself upward with all his strength.

At that moment the cold struck again.

This time Scott had his eyes wide open as the world he had known was replaced by the gray, dead landscape of nightmare. The stone of the hillside became a mass of twisted, torn flesh. The night sky burned with a sullen volcanic light, and the air filled with smells of sulfur and smoke. As Scott watched, the flesh shrank from Dee's body, leaving behind only dry bone.

"Scott!" Dee's voice cried from the skeleton face.

For an instant Scott thought that even on the fleshless skull he could read a feeling of terror. Under his fingers he felt Dee's hand melted down to knobby bone. Cold bone.

Then they plummeted down together.

The board made a pure, almost musical note as it cracked against the skull of the Umbra follower.

Harley raised the length of wood over her head, ready to strike again, but there was no need. The woman in the robe stumbled forward a step, fell to her knees, then toppled over on her face.

Harley looked around quickly. The woman had been one of the last crossing between the buildings, and nobody else was around to see her go down.

The woman moaned as Harley grabbed the edge of her robe and started to tug it over the unconscious woman's head.

"Shhh," warned Harley. "I need this."

She managed to pull the robe free. In less than a minute Harley was back on her feet and wearing the purple robe. She reached down, grabbed the Umbra woman by her ankles, and dragged her toward the shadows of a nearby building. She was almost finished when another robed figure approached. Harley tensed, but the figure raised a sleeve and waved.

"It's me," said Kenyon. He pushed the cowl of his robe back enough that Harley could see a shadow of his face. "Looks like you found a disguise."

Harley nodded. "These people might be spooky, but they're not too tough one-on-one."

"That would be a comfort if we only had to take

out one or two," said Kenyon. He raised his right hand, and the dark end of his pistol slipped out from beneath the material of his robe. "Let's just hope this is enough to make the whole crowd think twice about fighting."

"I'm hoping they don't even know we're here," Harley replied. "Let's get Dee and Scott and get out of this place."

Together they started across the compound along the path that had been worn down by the passage of the crowd. Walking along in the dark embrace of the purple robe, Harley felt cold sweat break out over her skin. Of all the things that had happened since her father's disappearance, her capture by Umbra had been the most terrifying. Escaping from their underground lair had nearly cost her life. Now she was about to walk back into their hands.

They were almost at the mouth of the canyon when a chorus of voices suddenly rose in a jerky, irregular song. Harley paused and tilted her head to one side as she listened. There was something familiar about the music. Hidden within its twisting, warped notes, Harley was sure she could pick out some old tune. She pushed back her hood so she could listen better and tapped her foot as she tried to find the hidden rhythm. She hummed a few notes. It was as haunting as a half-forgotten memory. Harley felt her body begin to sway as the music swelled inside her head.

A hand touched her shoulder. "Can I ask what you're doing?" Kenyon hissed.

Harley opened her mouth to explain, then felt a flush of embarrassment. "I was just . . . listening to the music."

Kenyon snorted. "I don't think I would call that

music." He reached to Harley's shoulder and tapped the folds of her hood. "You better put this back on unless you want to fight the whole bunch."

Harley quickly grabbed the folds of cloth and tugged it over her head. "Right."

"You sure you're okay?"

"Absolutely." Harley could still hear the music trying to get into her thoughts. She shook her head quickly. "Let's get moving."

Only a few more steps took them to the mouth of the box canyon where the ceremony was being held. At first Harley could see only flickering, chaotic shadows. Then she was able to make out a circle of bodies shuffling around a small fire. There was someone standing at the center of the circle and some sort of device resting on a cart. The air above the circle seemed to waver and glisten like the air above the highway on a hot summer day.

"Can you see where they have Dee and Scott?" she whispered.

"Not yet," Kenyon replied. He took another step forward. "Wait. There!" He pointed toward the twisting mass of people. "On the right side. See them?"

Harley stared hard. She thought she did see . . . something. "Are you sure?"

"No," Kenyon replied instantly. "Let's go closer."

The music grew louder and more insane as they drew near the circling crowd. Several times Harley had to fight to keep the notes from pressing their way into her mind. A string of darting melody ran across her thoughts, and her feet took an involuntary jump as the music seeped into her bones. She reached into her hood and pressed her palms against her forehead. "Twinkle, twinkle, little star," she mumbled under her breath. "How I wonder—"

Kenyon leaned in close. "Are you okay?"

Harley nodded. With the simple tune of the old nursery rhyme repeating in her head, she started forward again.

The small fire in the middle of the circle cast a reddish glow through the crowd. The dancing people didn't seem to notice the two intruders moving outside their circle of light. Harley and Kenyon were careful to keep in the shadows, at least twenty yards back from the edge of the circle, but Harley didn't think it would matter if they were to walk right through the center of the group. From close by it was obvious that the people in the circle had gone completely mad.

The Umbra members leaped into the air and landed only to leap again. Some rolled on the ground. Others clawed at their own flesh as if it were on fire. What had seemed like one vast song broke down at close range into screaming and sobbing and the mad cawing of a hundred throats. The ground shook with their noise, and the canyon walls threw back echoes that merged and amplified the chaos still more.

The objects that Kenyon had spotted from a distance became clear as they closed in—two tall wooden posts that had been planted in the dry ground. None of the dancers stood within a dozen yards of the posts. All of them seemed far more intent on their mad music than any prisoners. Harley hurried around the last few yards and came up to one of the wooden poles.

It was empty. Loose cords dangled from heavy bolts set into the rough wood, but they held no one. Harley started toward the second post and almost immediately saw that a prisoner was bound to the wood. Harley saw pale skin, and a small body, and tousled auburn hair. It was Dee Janes.

Harley's heart fell like a stone. Dee sagged bonelessly against the ropes holding her to the wooden post. Her head fell limp against her chest, and her limbs were bound tight against the planks. Harley stopped where she stood, caught between the desire to go up and check to see if Dee was all right and the terrible fear of what she might learn. Dee looked so . . . lifeless.

Kenyon didn't hesitate. He stepped past Harley and went straight to Dee. He pressed his palm under her chin and tipped Dee's head back. Then he placed a finger against her throat. Even in the faint red glow of the fire Harley could clearly see the dark circle of bruises around Dee's neck, and for a moment she was certain that Dee was dead.

"She's alive," Kenyon said. He spoke loudly to be heard over the din of the Umbra ceremony.

Harley closed her eyes in thanks, then quickly inspected the ropes holding Dee to the rough wood. "What about Scott?" she asked as she fumbled at the first knot. "Do you see him?"

Kenyon shook his head. "He has to be around here somewhere. We'll find him."

Dee Janes suddenly raised her head. She mumbled something, but her voice was a harsh, choked whisper.

Her words were lost against the noise of the circle.

Harley leaned down and brought her face close to Dee's. "What is it?" she asked.

"Scott," Dee whispered. "Watch . . . Scott."

"We're looking for him now," Harley replied. She finished untying the knots holding Dee's right hand and started on the left. "Don't worry. We'll find him."

"No!" Dee replied with surprising strength. "Watch *out* for Scott. He's changed."

Harley frowned. "Changed? Changed how?"

The answer came from behind Harley. She heard a groan, then a sharp crack. She spun around to see Kenyon crumple to the ground. Close by stood a tall figure that was dressed in the torn remains of jeans and a T-shirt that had been split open at the seams. The face above the ripped shirt was no face at all— only a silhouette of absolute darkness.

Harley took a quick step back. She had fought against the shadow men more than once, and she knew better than to face the thing without a weapon. She glanced at Kenyon's fallen form. Regular guns didn't seem to have much effect on the creatures, but if Harley could get Kenyon's pistol she might be able to slow the thing down. With her eyes fixed on the tall, dark figure she took a careful step toward Kenyon.

"Hello, Harley," said the shadow man.

Harley froze. The voice of the shadow man was deep and echoing but also horribly familiar. Gooseflesh broke out on Harley's arms. "Scott?" she whispered. "Is that you?"

The unseen face nodded. "It's me. Or it was me. I'm not sure."

Harley swallowed hard. "How did this happen?"

Scott raised a midnight hand and flexed his fingers. "It's power," he said. "Pure power. I . . ." For a moment the towering figure seemed to sag. It lost height and bulk, and the blanket of pure night fell away. For a few seconds Harley could see Scott's thin features through the veil of shadow. His face was twisted in agony.

Harley trembled. "Scott, what should I do? How can we make you better?"

Scott opened his mouth, but before he could reply, the covering of darkness returned. "I am better," he growled in his new, deep voice. "You're the one that doesn't look so good." There was a hint of awful laughter in the rumbling voice.

Harley wasn't sure what Scott was talking about, but she was sure that the change in him was more than how he looked. She could feel the icy cold rolling from his shadowy form. Once again she edged toward Kenyon.

"Don't even try," said Scott. He stepped forward, bent down, and picked up Kenyon's gun. White frost spread quickly over the gleaming metal. With a snap like a breaking twig the frozen gun cracked into two pieces and thudded to the ground. Scott turned toward the circle of figures that was still dancing and singing wildly. "We have visitors," he called.

At once a small robed form stepped from the center of the circle. "I know," said a calm voice. With a fluid gesture the figure swept back her hood and revealed beautiful smooth features surrounded by a wealth of flowing golden hair. "I assume this is Kathleen Davisidaro."

"Yes," answered Scott. "She came to try and rescue Dee."

"How sweet," said the woman in the robe. "I'm sure that she also had your best interest at heart." She looked at Harley and smiled. "I'm Chloe Adair," she said. "I'm afraid we didn't get the chance to be introduced when I came to collect Scott. It's so nice that we have another chance to meet."

Harley felt a soft vise close around her head and begin to squeeze. Her thoughts grew jumbled. "What . . . what are you doing?"

"Doing?" Chloe frowned prettily. "I have no idea what you mean."

The pressure on Harley's skull increased, and sparks of color flickered across her vision. Something was pushing into her mind, pressing through her thoughts like needles of cold steel. Harley clamped her hands to the side of her head. "Get out," she muttered. "Get out!" The pressure in her mind eased.

Chloe laughed. "It seems your friend Harley does have some power." She folded her arms and looked at Harley with a smug expression. "Not enough to matter, of course."

Harley looked past her to the thing that had been Scott Handleson. "Scott, I don't know what she's done to you, but you have to know this is wrong. Dee loves you. Kenyon's your best friend. You have to help them."

Chloe laughed again, her sharp musical tones cutting through the noise of the wild dance. "You're wasting your time. Scott was mine even before he took up the dark cloak. Legion bred him to be my servant. It's his destiny."

Harley ignored her. She stepped toward Scott and held out her hands. "Dee loves you, Scott. Really loves you." She looked into the empty dark face. "Doesn't that mean something?"

Chloe stepped around Scott and stood between him and Harley. "That's enough talking from you," she said. She raised one pale hand and gave a smooth, delicate gesture.

At once the sharp pressure returned to Harley's mind. She staggered and raised her hands to her aching head. "Scott . . . ," she tried again, but the pressure swelled until it choked away all control of her speech. All at once every muscle in her body seemed to turn to jelly. The ground leaped up and slapped her hard across the face. Dizzy and confused, Harley looked up to see Chloe and the thing that had been Scott standing over her.

"Just stay right there," said Chloe, "and keep watching. We're almost at the end now—you wouldn't want to miss it."

With tremendous effort Harley forced out a sentence. "The end of what?"

"The end of the world," Chloe said brightly. "Won't that be fun?" She turned and glided smoothly away.

Scott walked away from the cluster of skeletons and followed Chloe across the squirming, worm-ridden ground. The sky overhead was an angry, boiling red.

He felt strange. Actually that wasn't quite true. He had just watched his friend be smashed to the ground and was about to watch the end of the world, and on top of that he had turned into some kind of monster. The really strange thing was that he *didn't* feel strange. In fact, he hardly felt anything at all. Pale ghosts of emotions sailed across his mind, but they were weak, distant phantoms.

Those are from another life, he thought. From when I was weak.

"It's time to start up your creation," said Chloe. She laughed briefly. "We start your creation, and we end this one."

Two moldering skeletons came forward from the circling crowd. Scott assumed that these things in the torn strips of robes were Drake and Alice, but it didn't really matter. Except for Chloe, all the things around him were the same.

One of the skeletons reached into the mass of sticks and meaningless trash that before the change had been Scott's machine. There was a click, and a point of white fire appeared in the center of the mass. Streamers of pale fire emerged from all the dancing, howling skeletons around the circle. The light swirled slowly into the machine, then out to Chloe. From there the light moved upward and began to form a cloud overhead. The machine was working.

Scott felt neither satisfaction nor regret. All his emotions were frozen in the cloud of darkness that cloaked his body.

Stop them.

Scott felt momentarily puzzled. He looked around for the source of the voice, but he saw only Chloe. The rest of the Umbra members were staying back at the edge of the circle.

Stop them, the voice repeated. *You can't let Chloe destroy everything.*

Scott realized that the voice wasn't coming from outside. It was in his own skull, his own mind. He barely gave the voice a second thought. Curiosity— like fear, anger, and love—was something for those that were not clothed in night.

It has to be you, said the strange internal voice. *Stop them.*

Why should I stop Chloe? Scott replied in his mind. He raised his shadowed face and looked up at the gathering storm of light. *Legion made me to help Chloe. I'm nothing but a machine.*

You're more than that.

Scott shook his head. The strange voice stirred up a faint glimmer of emotion—a blue trace of guilt and regret—but he shoved it away. There was no need for those things now. Scott had his coldness. As long as he held tight to the empty black heart of darkness, he could never again be bitten by disappointment or loss. *I'm nothing but a robot. I was Legion's robot. Now I'm Chloe's robot. I can do nothing.*

You have to, the voice insisted. *You're the only one who can stop them.*

The voice had a certainty that Scott couldn't ever remember feeling. In a completely different way the voice seemed as perfect as the darkness at the heart of the shadows.

Who are you? thought Scott. *What are you?*

Before the voice could answer, Chloe let out an excited cry. "The sphere is forming!" she shouted. "I've done it!"

The white cloud overhead spun and pulled together like the birth of a star. It collapsed into a sphere of light at least ten feet across. The white glare seemed to cut through the stone of the canyon like the world's largest x ray, baring the very roots of the earth.

Chloe jumped into the air and clapped with uncontrollable joy. For a moment her usual grace left her, and she seemed like any excited teenager—like a girl who had discovered that her parents had bought her a car for her birthday.

"Now!" she screamed. "Now the ancient ones will come. It's time! It's finally time!"

All around Scott the dancing skeletons paused. He glanced over at the bony forms that represented Kenyon, Dee, and Harley. Kenyon was still sprawled on the ground, and Dee was still fixed to the post—a bone post to Scott's eyes—but Harley was on her feet, facing the forming sphere. No one bothered to guard them. There was no need.

Slowly the white sphere settled to the ground. Scott and Chloe stepped back as the sphere consumed the small fire at the center of the circle. Scott watched as a gray shadow flickered through the bright heart of the white globe.

"Come forth!" Chloe cried into the light. "We await your coming!" Behind her the ranks of Umbra fell absolutely still and silent.

The shape in the sphere turned, twisted, then came clear. Out of the ball of light stepped a young man with broad shoulders and rough, homemade clothing. He stumbled onto the sandy ground and shielded his eyes against the light.

"Hi," he said. "I'm home."

SEVENTEEN

"Noah!" Harley shouted in astonishment.

Noah Templer looked just the same as he had when Harley had seen him in the dream world, right down to the tattered vest and the wide hat perched on his head. But this wasn't a dream. Noah was real. He was back.

He stood in the center of the circle with the white sphere behind him. The ball of brilliant light spread Noah's shadow across the dry ground and surrounded Noah in a halo of fire. Around him the gathering of Umbra members stood in silent shock. To Harley, Noah looked like some kind of supernatural creature come to put a stop to this gathering—an angel in a leather vest.

Harley took one tentative step toward him, then another. A moment later she was running. She ignored Chloe, the shadow men, and the silent ranks of Umbra members gathered around the circle as she rushed over the hard dry ground toward Noah.

"Stop her!" Chloe cried. "Don't let them get together!"

Hands reached toward Harley from all sides. She dodged away from a tall man in a robe and slipped loose from the grip of another Umbra member. A shadow man lurched forward, and Harley made a quick step right to avoid the dark hands that reached out toward her. But as she dodged the shadow man another figure dashed in from her right. Strong hands closed on Harley's arm and held her firmly. She turned to see another man in a robe. Inside his hood a long curving scar marked his face.

"Be still," he said in a calm professional voice. "We don't want to hurt you."

"Yes, we do!" screeched Chloe. Her face, which had been glowing with ecstasy at the opening of the sphere, was now twisted in rage. "The time for being calm and gentle is past! These people are blocking our route to the old ones. We want to hurt them both— we want to *destroy* them."

Noah Templer stepped away from the center of the circle. Behind him the sphere of light grew smaller and dimmer. It took on a pearl gray color and swam with hints of a thousand hues. "Leave her alone!" Noah demanded in a strong voice.

A ripple ran through the circle of Umbra members like trees being blown by an autumn wind. Harley felt something, too. A fresh surge of power had entered the circle, and she had no doubt about the source. "Noah!" she called to him. "There are shadow men. Be careful."

"Don't worry, Harley," he replied. "The shadow men aren't the problem." Noah stepped away from the center of the light. As he moved from the glare of the sphere Harley's heart fell. There was exhaustion written into every line of Noah's face. His strong features were drawn and haggard, and his bare chest was slick with sweat between the edges of the vest. He moved stiffly, as if he were carrying some great weight on his back. Still he managed to raise his face and look at Chloe with a determined expression. "Let Harley go and move away," he said.

Chloe looked at him with a smirk on her too pretty face. "What if I don't?" she asked. She strolled slowly toward the center of the circle with an easy grace, like a princess crossing a ballroom. "Are you going to make me?"

"I'll do what I have to," said Noah. He trembled. Beads of sweat rolled down his face and dripped from the point of his chin.

"Oh, how fearful!" Chloe clapped and laughed. "Look at you. It took almost everything you had to cross through the gate, didn't it?"

Noah didn't reply. As Harley watched, his face grew darker and the muscles of his jaw tightened. It was as if he were holding up some tremendous weight.

"Even now you're spending the last of your reserves just to hold the gate," said Chloe. "Do you think you can fight me?"

The cords of Noah's neck were stretched tight, and his shoulder muscles bunched and quivered. "Get back," he said through clenched teeth. "You don't know what's in there."

Chloe laughed. "I know exactly what's in there," she said. "This is what I've been waiting for."

Harley jerked against the grip of the man holding her and managed to drag him forward a few steps. "Noah!" she called. She wanted to go to him, to help him, but she didn't even completely understand what was happening.

Noah suddenly reached into the air. A smear of color appeared between his hands. With lightning speed the color lengthened, gathered substance, and became a glowing silver bow complete with a white-feathered arrow. Noah lowered his hands. "End this now," he called in a strained voice. "Or I will."

One of the shadow men moved toward Noah, but Chloe waved the creature back. She took a step toward Noah, pushed her chest forward, and put her hands behind her back. "Aim carefully," she said. "Right through the heart."

Harley saw a moment of doubt cross Noah's face, but it was gone as quickly as it came. He lowered the silver bow and pointed the gleaming tip of the arrow toward Chloe. With a swift movement of his right hand he caught the back of the arrow and drew back the bowstring. "Last chance," he called through gritted teeth. "I'll use this if I—"

Suddenly the silver bow folded in half, then crumpled like a wad of damp paper. Noah cried out and let the would-be weapon fall from his hands. Halfway to the ground the bow disappeared in a smear of silver streaks.

"Oh, my," said Chloe. "I wonder what went wrong?"

Noah's face was caught in astonishment and despair. "How did you do that?"

"I did nothing," Chloe replied. She walked closer to him, the hem of her robe brushing softly over the ground.

As she neared Noah, Harley noticed something for the first time—Chloe and Noah looked alike. It was more than a casual resemblance. They both had wavy blond hair, bright blue eyes, and clean, regular features. Noah was several inches taller, and Chloe's face held a softer, female beauty, but there was no mistaking the similarity between them.

It's a *family* resemblance, Harley realized suddenly. It was something she should have realized before. Noah and Chloe were both products of the Legion breeding program, and they had both been created through generations of effort aimed at producing human beings with intense mental powers. In a way Noah and Chloe were Legion's ultimate creations—the male and female versions of perfect human beings. Scott had once said he thought of Chloe as his sister, but it was Noah and Chloe that were as close—or closer—than any siblings. The revelation left Harley gasping.

Chloe walked in slow circles around Noah, like a matador stalking a bull. "You'll find that bending reality isn't so easy on this side of the gate," she said. "Within the sphere your own mind provided the template for what went on around you. Out here the world isn't nearly so clean."

Noah pressed his lips together and raised a hand. Colors flowed around him again as something began to form.

"Enough games!" shouted Chloe. She made a swift gesture with her arms, and the color gathering around Noah was blown away like thistledown before a stiff wind. "Move away and release your hold on the gate."

"I can't." Noah shook his head. Behind him a fresh wave of colors passed over the shrunken sphere. "If I let it go, they'll come through."

Chloe nodded. "Exactly." She raised her right hand and cupped her fingers as if she were gripping a baseball.

At once a small sphere of deep red light formed against her palm. With an almost casual gesture she flipped the sphere toward Noah.

"No!" Harley shouted. She tore free of the man holding her and ran toward Noah.

Without even looking around, Chloe summoned a second red sphere and tossed it toward Harley. It transformed into a red streak that lanced through the night air and struck Harley like a charging elephant. Harley was blasted from the ground and flung a dozen feet through the air. She landed facedown in the sand with her ears ringing and her vision filled with sparks. On trembling arms she raised herself up and looked toward the center of the circle.

Noah was on his knees. His mouth hung open, and sweat dripped from his upraised arms like rain falling from the branches of a tree. Even from a distance she could see the veins standing out at his temples and throat.

In front of him Chloe stood perfectly composed. "Submit," she said. She held out her hand, and another sphere formed. "You can release your hold on the gate, or I can kill you and take it."

Noah gave a deep, despairing cry. His hands clenched into fists, and his eyes rolled up until only the whites were showing. "I can't," he groaned.

"But you must," said Chloe. She sent the red sphere flashing toward him.

Crimson light washed over Noah. Smoke rose from his leather vest, and red sparks danced along his bared teeth. For a moment he remained on his knees, then he swayed and fell to his side in the dust.

Chloe stepped past him without a second glance. "Enough interruptions," she said. She looked toward the white sphere. At once the ball brightened and widened. The swimming colors were washed away in torrents of agonizing brightness. And from somewhere deep inside the sphere something moved—something that twisted, and quivered, and swelled.

Harley looked at Noah's body lying on the ground and felt familiar rage replacing her despair. Red pain swirled in her head and the world swayed around her, but she got to her feet. Kenyon and Dee were out of the picture. Scott had become a monster, and now Noah lay in the dust. It was up to her. With no real thought for what she was going to do, she ran toward the center of the circle.

Before Harley had taken ten steps, Chloe whirled around. The blond girl's eyes literally glowed with a blue-white fire. "It appears you aren't smart enough to stay out of my way. I suppose I'll just have to kill you." She raised her hand, and a new red sphere began to form.

Harley skidded to a halt. She looked left and right, but there was only the gathered circle of Umbra members. There were no weapons, no allies, and no escape routes. She stood up straight and faced Chloe. "Why?" she asked.

"Why kill you?" Chloe shrugged. "It's easier that way—not to mention more fun."

"No," Harley said with a shake of her head. "Why open the gate? Why let these things Noah warned you about into our world?"

"Rules," replied Chloe.

"What?" Harley asked in confusion.

"Rules," Chloe repeated. She let the red ball in her hand evaporate and turned to reach out to the large sphere of white. Whatever was inside the sphere was drawing close. Its inhuman form was becoming clearer and more disturbing with each passing second. "This world is built from rules," she said. "That's the way it is because that's the way we *think* it is."

The string of words left Harley shaking her head. "What does that mean?"

Chloe laughed her deceptively sweet musical laugh. "I wouldn't expect you to understand," she said. "Just think of everything around you as part of a great, long dream—a dream we all share. But when the ancient ones return to our sphere . . ." Chloe's voice faded away, and she shivered. For a moment Harley thought the Umbra leader was afraid, then she saw the wide smile on Chloe's face. The shiver wasn't fear. It was ecstasy.

"When the ancient ones return," Chloe continued, "the long dream is over."

Harley didn't need anyone to explain what the words meant. Two things were suddenly quite clear. First, if the things inside the sphere escaped into reality, it might mean the end of the world. And second— Chloe Adair was completely insane. Harley scanned the circle again, desperately looking for some way to stop what was happening. Her eyes settled on a tall, midnight figure a dozen feet behind Chloe.

Scott Handleson still wore the remnants of his clothing, but there seemed to be no remaining sign of his humanity. His face and flesh were gone, cased in deep, impenetrable shadow. Harley glanced back at Chloe. "You don't like rules."

"I hate rules." Chloe tossed her head, and sparks of blue light flew from her glowing eyes. "When the ancient ones arrive, all the rules will finally be lifted."

"But what about Legion's rules?" asked Harley. "Can you break them?"

Chloe sneered. "Legion doesn't make rules for me."

Harley frowned. "The Legion agent we found back in Stone Harbor—he was your protector, wasn't he?"

"Yes."

"And you killed him."

"Oh yes." Chloe closed her eyes, momentarily hiding the fire inside. She ran the pink tip of her tongue across her lips. "He won't be making any rules for me."

Harley stepped toward her. "But I thought Legion bred your kind and the protectors to be partners. You're not supposed to kill them."

Chloe shook her head. "It doesn't matter what Legion planned for me. I'm no robot. I don't follow their rules."

At that moment something emerged from the sphere. It was a long, many-jointed feeler—like the antenna of an insect. Only this antenna was at least six feet long and ended in a cluster of yawning pink mouths. The mouths opened and began to bawl like kittens in pain.

"They're here!" Chloe shouted in excitement. "Dance, everyone! It's time to dance!" Behind her there was more stirring within the sphere. The ancient ones were coming through.

EIGHTEEN

Chloe reached out to Scott's dark fingers. "Dance!" she cried. "Dance to greet the ancient ones!" She tugged on his icy hand, but Scott felt no urge to celebrate. Chloe released her grip and whirred away, circling and leaping madly.

Scott watched her with no feeling. Before his transformation, he would have been thrilled at her touch. Before his transformation, he would have been horrified at the things he had seen in the circle. But neither horror nor desire could strike him free of the cold, dark circle where his soul now lived.

He watched without emotion as the thing unfolded from the sphere. Scott knew that his vision was different from those that weren't masked by shadow, but he had a feeling that—like Chloe—the things in the sphere looked the same from any reality. A wrinkled, swaying tube emerged from the light—like an elephant's trunk but lined with gleaming dark spikes. A milky white eye on a limp stalk flopped out of the sphere and lay pulsing on the ground. It cried dark, foul-smelling tears.

All around the circle the Umbra members were joining Chloe in the wild dance. The ground shook with the movement of their feet and the air rang with their chants as they welcomed the ancient ones into the world. But even the joy of the ceremony was denied to Scott. He wondered if it would be the same for him even after the ancient ones had spilled into the world. The rest of the world might give way to terror and madness, but for him there would be only the cold and dark. Forever.

"Scott," said a voice at his back.

He turned slowly and found himself staring at a ghost. A ghost of Scott Handleson.

"You're not real," he said in his new, rumbling voice.

"I am," replied the ghost. "I'm just as real as you. And I need your help." The specter raised one hand and pointed across the circle. "You have to stop Chloe now, before things get any worse."

A phantom of emotion stirred in Scott's thoughts, but it was gone before he could name it. "I can do nothing."

"You can."

"I don't care," Scott replied slowly. "Stay away from me. You're not part of me anymore." He turned away from the specter.

The ghost of his old self spoke from behind him. "You know that's not true. You do care what's happening."

Scott shook his shadowy head. "I serve the Ipolex. If this is what she wants to do, then I have no choice."

"Even if it means killing Dee?"

Killing Dee. The words echoed through Scott's mind with unexpected weight. He made a slow turn and looked toward the tall poles of bone on the edge of the circle. Bound by the rough length of rope, a small skeleton sagged against one of the poles. It was a worthless thing, a thing of death and bones. Like everything else in the cold, dark world of the shadow man, it was both ugly and pitiful. But Scott knew that what he saw through shadow was not all there was.

Dee was no collection of rotting bones. Dee was fun, and brave, and wonderfully alive.

Another tinge of emotion passed through him. No genetic code had ever told him to love Dee Janes. He remembered the girl he knew—the round face, her soft brown eyes, her smooth auburn hair. The Dee who was always ready with a joke. The Dee who was so much prettier than she knew.

Slowly an image seemed to form over the scene of bones and death. He could see Dee—the real Dee. And with that vision came a mingling of love and fear. The emotions were like a single patch of blue sky breaking through a cloudy day, and almost immediately they threatened to disappear behind the banks of darkness. Scott struggled to hold on to the light.

"What do I do?" he asked. His own voice made him feel a shiver of helplessness. It was deep, hollow, and rolling—a shadow man's voice, not the voice of a human being.

The ghost looked up at him with hope etched on the transparent features of his face. "You've written computer programs for years," he said. "But this time you need to *crash* one."

189

NINETEEN

Harley watched in horror as more of the creature emerged from the sphere. She remembered the thing that had lived in the pit beneath Umbra's underground headquarters. The creature struggling from the sphere wasn't the same, but it was from the same awful family.

As more of the creature slid through the sphere Harley felt the air around her grow strangely thick. The sky overhead took on tones of pink and green. The ground quivered.

It's happening, she thought. The thing is only halfway into our world, and already reality is starting to break down.

There was a groan from near her feet. Harley looked down and was overjoyed to see Noah Templer rubbing at the side of his head. She dropped to her knees beside him. "I thought you were dead."

"So did I," said Noah. He raised his head and looked at the thing coming out of the sphere. "Though it looks like we might be right in a few minutes."

"If we had a gun . . . ," started Harley.

Noah shook his head. "It wouldn't matter. I don't think a bazooka would even slow that thing down."

Harley put an arm around Noah and helped him to his feet. Together they turned to face the end of the world.

Chloe danced wildly in front of the emerging beast. Her small hands darted out to touch the quivering antenna, and her fingers slipped between the spines to hold the wiggling trunk. Changing reality shifted over her. She metamorphosed from a beautiful girl into a thing almost as twisted as the creature she handled. Her arms became sharp and jagged, covered in glistening green plates—like the arms of a huge praying mantis. The robe slipped away to reveal a body made from a thousand twisting snakes. Only her face and hair remained unchanged—as if her head had been grafted onto the obscenely wriggling mass.

"Yes!" she cried in a slurred, rippling voice. "No rules! No more rules!" All around the circle the minions of Umbra gave an answering shout. People began to crowd forward, moving toward the thing that had been their leader as if they expected to receive a blessing.

Harley raised a hand and shielded herself from the sight. She could feel the world around her shaking, as if every atom and every rule of physics were teetering on the edge of madness. The thought of a whole world transformed in the image of these horrors was sickening.

Suddenly a tall black form forced its way through the circling crowd and stalked straight toward Harley. Harley stumbled back a step before she recognized the torn remains of its clothing. "Scott?"

The shadow man stood still for a moment. "Tell Dee," said the well-deep voice. "Tell Dee she saved me."

Harley shook her head. "Dee saved you? What do you mean?"

Without replying, Scott turned and lurched toward the center of the circle. He had taken two long strides before Harley realized what he meant to do. "Scott!" she shouted. "No!"

But it was too late for any warnings. Scott walked around the creature's probing snout and stood over the thing that had once been a girl.

Chloe Adair's face looked up at him from her perch atop a mass of writhing, snapping serpents. "No more rules, Scott," she called in her distorted voice. "Remember how much I hated the rules back at the orphanage? Well, that's all over now!"

Scott nodded. "Yes," he replied. "All over." He bent and gathered the squirming thing into his arms.

A look of rage twisted Chloe's disembodied face. "Put me down!"

"No." Scott kicked the probing antenna aside and took a step toward the sphere.

"You can't hurt me," screamed Chloe. "It's against your programming."

Scott hesitated on the lip of the white sphere. "I'm not a robot," he said. "I don't have a program." Then he stepped into the sphere.

The next second was taken up by the explosion.

The blast threw Harley to the ground and peppered her with bits of sand and rock. The white sphere flashed out of existence, leaving behind the severed end of a spiny trunk and a five-foot section of antenna that twisted and jerked like an angry serpent. Most of the Umbra members were flattened by the explosion. Others screamed and ran madly into the darkness. Even the shadow men groaned and shuffled around the circle.

Harley struggled to her feet and ran toward the site

of the blast. "Scott!" A shallow depression had been cut in the ground where the sphere rested. It was black and smooth and shiny as glass. There was no sign of Scott or Chloe.

A hand landed on her shoulder, and Harley jumped. "He's gone," said Noah.

Harley shook her head. "There's got to be something we can do."

"Not here," Noah replied. "Not now. Trust me, I know about the sphere."

Harley looked at the mad scene around them. Dozens of Umbra members lay weeping on the ground while others tore at their robes and cried out. She saw two shadow men struggling together like wrestlers. "Now what?"

Noah took her by the arm and turned her toward the place where Kenyon and Dee waited at the edge of the circle. "Now we get out of here before these people wake up and blame us for what happened."

They hurried through the milling crowd to find that Kenyon was already awake and working to free Dee. He looked up as Harley and Noah approached. For a moment Harley saw relief spread across Kenyon's face as he looked at her.

"You're all right!" he cried. "I thought the explosion—" His eyes slid up toward Noah, and the excited look on his face was replaced by his usual cool expression. "Come and help me untie Dee. I'm almost done."

Dee seemed only half awake, but tears streamed down her face. "Scott," she sobbed.

Harley tried her best to hold Dee while Noah

joined Kenyon in loosening the ropes. "He said you saved him," she said softly.

Dee shook her head. "No. He saved *me*. He saved us all."

Kenyon gave a sharp tug on a rope. "There," he said. "That should—"

A chain saw whine sounded through the canyon. Sparks rained off the rock walls, and a dozen Umbra members fell among screams and shouts.

"Get down!" Kenyon shouted. "It's Unit 17!"

All four of them hit the ground as the whine of Unit 17's weapons increased. Harley almost felt like laughing as the volume of the gunfire ramped up and up. First Umbra, then Unit 17. It was all too much.

"Over there!" Noah pointed to the left. "Those rocks will give us some cover."

Harley was none too sure the rocks were the right place to protect them from Unit 17, but she followed as everyone crawled rapidly behind the meager cover.

Kenyon threw himself down at Harley's side. "I don't understand how Unit 17 tracked us here," he said as one of the weapons chipped into the stone above their heads. "Abel said that they followed the microprobes on the van, and we left the van behind a long time ago."

"Who's Abel?" asked Noah.

Harley started to explain, but a fresh round of firing drowned out her words.

A shadow man ran past their position. So many of the Umbra shots struck its midnight body that it twitched and jerked like a bag of popcorn in the microwave. Its robe was torn to tatters. But the shadow man kept running.

"Unit 17 is going to have their hands full with those things," said Kenyon.

"Somehow I don't feel sorry for either of them," Noah replied.

Dee crawled up between Harley and Kenyon. "Guys, I want to go home," she said weakly.

"If we break cover, we're going to take a lot of fire," Kenyon warned. "I doubt we'd make it ten steps down that canyon before we were all dead."

Noah scooted along on elbows and knees to join the others. "Not necessarily," he said. He ran his hand through his tangled blond hair. "I may not be able to make a working weapon, but I think I can still manage an illusion."

A moment later a shape began to form in front of the stones they were using for cover. At first it was just the rough outline of a person, but with each passing second it looked more solid and detailed. After ten seconds a passable image of Noah stood among the boulders.

"What do you think?" asked Noah.

Kenyon nodded. "That should draw some fire." As if to punctuate his words, a fresh round of shots cut through the shadow-Noah. The shots passed through the illusion and slammed into the rocks beyond.

"Now for the rest," said Noah. Within a minute the image of Noah had been joined by shades of Dee, Kenyon, and Harley. The illusions drew steady fire from the Unit 17 guns.

Noah pointed to the canyon wall. "There's some sage back there. If we crawl in and hide, we might wait this whole thing out while the illusions lead them out of the area."

Harley followed the direction Noah was pointing and frowned. The sagebrush was thin and separated by patches of bare earth. But there didn't seem to be any better option. "All right," she said. "Let's do it."

Kenyon shook his head. "No," he said firmly.

Harley looked at him in surprise. "Why not?"

"Because. Until we know how Unit 17 tracked us to this place, we'll be sitting ducks." He nodded to the four shadowy images in front of the rocks. "A lot of good these illusions will do if they've got one of their probes on us."

A memory suddenly came to Harley. She remembered Abel telling them about the microprobes, and how she had gotten close to Kenyon, and a flash of golden glitter. "Take off your shirt," she said to Kenyon.

Kenyon scowled. "What?"

"Your shirt," Harley repeated. "Abel covered it in microprobes. That's how they're finding us."

"Why would she do that?"

Harley gestured at the chaos beyond the rocks. Umbra members were running and screaming. Bodies littered the ground. Unit 17 guns fired in all directions. Shadow men lumbered about in the remains of robes. "She did it because this is what she wanted all along," said Harley. "Abel was using us to bring Umbra and Unit 17 together."

Kenyon scowled. "The next time I see Ms. Abel, I think we're going to have a very long talk." He peeled off his black sweater and tossed it out over the rocks.

"There. I sure hope you're right about this." He turned and started crawling toward the sage.

Harley was about to follow, but Dee reached out and grabbed her by the wrist.

"Wait," she said. "It's not right." Dee pointed to the illusions and then turned to Noah. "Scott should be out there with us."

Noah winced. "Dee, I didn't know Scott very well. The first time I saw him, I was mostly out of it. And this time, well, you don't want to remember him that way."

"Just try," Dee urged.

Noah nodded. "All right." He closed his eyes. In a moment a tall, thin figure had joined the other illusions.

Dee surveyed his work for a moment and nodded. "There," she said. "Now it looks right." She turned and crawled away toward the bushes.

Harley hesitated for a moment. The five images lined in front of the stones were beginning to waver. She suspected that Noah's illusions would soon weaken and fade.

They're not going to last, she thought. But then again, nothing does. She dug her elbows into the hard, sandy soil and crawled after the others.

EPILOGUE

From the top of the stone tower, Harley could see for a hundred miles. Tourist cars crept along the roads of the national monument like ants on the trail of a picnic. The corrugated metal roof of the park visitor center shimmered in the sun like a distant lake. Farther away she could just make out vehicles and homes within the boundaries of the Lakota reservation.

I wonder if they knew what was happening? she thought. Did some old medicine man or wisewoman give a prophecy about this? If they had, the Lakota hadn't done anything about it. Of course, the prophecy might have told them it was all going to work out without their help. A few months ago Harley would have thought it was silly to even think about such things as prophecies. Now she believed. She believed in everything.

"Hey!" called a voice from the bottom of the tower. "You better come down from there before you fall!"

Harley leaned out and looked down to see Noah standing among the stony debris at the base of the steep slope. "You come up," she said. "There's room for two."

She waited while Noah made his way up the spire of pastel-colored stone. He pulled himself onto the ledge where Harley was sitting and leaned back against the rock. "You do have a good view from up here," he said.

Harley nodded. "Is Dee okay?"

"Not yet," Noah replied, "but she's getting there. She got hold of her father. Kenyon's already made arrangements to have her fly home from Rapid City this afternoon. Kenyon has his own ticket for Chicago."

Harley glanced over at Noah. He had changed the rough clothing of his private world for a cheap tourist T-shirt and jeans. Somehow the everyday clothing no longer looked right on him. He seemed more at home in his vest and leather.

"What about us?" Harley asked. "Where do we go from here?"

Noah slid closer and slipped an arm around her waist. "Wherever you want," he said. "There's nothing left for me in Stone Harbor. If you want to go with Kenyon, we can do that." He paused and looked at her. "Or you can go with him and I can go someplace else, if that's what you want."

"No," Harley replied. "That's definitely not what I want." She leaned against Noah's broad chest. "You've been away for a long time. I want you with me."

"I'm all for that."

There was silence for long seconds as Harley stared out toward the distant swell of the Black Hills. "He's gone," she said softly. "Isn't he?"

"Scott?" Noah shrugged. "It's hard to say. Of course, even if—"

"Not Scott. My father."

"Oh." Noah frowned and looked down at his dangling feet. "He was forced out of the first sphere, but that doesn't mean he's really gone. He's still out there somewhere. Maybe the next time someone cranks up a sphere, your dad will pop right through."

Harley nodded. "But with Unit 17's bases all busted and Umbra torn apart, there's not much chance anyone will be making a sphere anytime soon." She drew a deep breath. "My father is gone."

Noah was silent for a moment, then he gave Harley a quick, strong hug. "We better get down from here. Kenyon said he was going to order supper without us if we didn't get back soon." He brought his lips close to Harley's ear and spoke in a conspiratorial whisper. "I don't know this guy very well, but he looks like the sort that might order snails for supper if we're not there to stop him."

Harley smiled. "He'll probably do it, anyway. Kenyon's hard to stop once he sets his mind to something." She lifted her chin and looked into Noah's blue eyes. "What do we do now?" she asked. "Do we go on with our lives? Do we get jobs and pretend that none of this ever happened?"

Noah shrugged. "It's too bad I can't make things here like I did inside the sphere. Then we wouldn't need jobs." He closed his eyes, and his face tightened in effort. Then he relaxed and opened his eyes with a smile. "I do think I'm getting better at it." He raised his hand and passed Harley a flower.

Harley studied it in wonder. It was like a dandelion but three times bigger than any she had ever seen. Delicate, wispy seeds fluttered in the warm, dry wind. "You made this?"

"Well . . ." Noah winced, then broke into a grin.

"Actually I picked it on the way up. There's a whole bunch of them about three ledges down." He leaned toward Harley and brought his lips close to her face. "I never had a chance to bring you flowers."

"We never had a chance for anything," said Harley. "Maybe we will now." She brought her lips up against his and raised her hands to wrap them around Noah's neck. With a hundred-foot drop below her feet, she closed her eyes and surrendered to a kiss.

ARCHWAY PAPERBACKS

EXTREME ZONE #8

PROOF OF PURCHASE OFFER

OFFICIAL RULES

1. To receive your free EXTREME ZONE baseball cap (approximate retail value: $8.00), submit this completed Official Entry Form and at least one Official Entry Form from either books 1, 2, 3, 4, 5, 6, or 7 (no copies allowed). Offer good only while supplies last. Allow 6-8 weeks for delivery. Send entries to the Archway Paperbacks/EZ Promotion, 13th Floor, 1230 Avenue of the Americas, NY, NY 10020.

2. The offer is open to residents of the U.S. and Canada. Void where prohibited. Employees of Simon & Schuster, Inc., its parent, subsidiaries, suppliers, affiliates, agencies, participating retailers, and their families living in the same household are not eligible. One EXTREME ZONE baseball cap per person. Offer expires 12/31/97.

3. Not responsible for lost, late, postage due or misdirected responses. Requests not complying with all offer requirements will not be honored. Any fraudulent submission will be prosecuted to the fullest extent permitted by law.